An Incident on the Gosport Ferry

An Incident on the Gosport Ferry

David Gary

CHAPLIN BOOKS

www.chaplinbooks.co.uk

This is a work of fiction. Although the novel uses real locations,
its characters and events are solely the invention of the author and
any resemblance to any person, living or dead, is purely
coincidental.

Front cover illustration: Wendy Saunders

ISBN: 978-1-911105-58-9

Chaplin Books
5 Carlton Way
Gosport PO12 1LN
02392 529020

INTRODUCTION

'Portsmouth' is exactly that – it's the mouth of a rather large port, and to get from one side to the other in years past has always been tedious and nowadays to go by road is a traffic nightmare. Gosport is on a peninsular, possessing in reality only two roads to transfer the frustrated traveller on and off. Most people have to leave the peninsular to work and now, since the closure of the military hospital at Haslar, also to attend hospital appointments over in Portsmouth. There is only a small cottage-style hospital now left serving the town. Gosport is also the largest town in Britain without a railway station.

The residents have a choice of going to Fareham to catch trains, or across to Portsmouth Harbour station for trains to Waterloo and other stations on the south coast. A ferry to Portsmouth from Gosport has always been a good idea and so, for as far back as we can trace, there have been ferry boats crossing the mouth of Portsmouth Harbour transporting people from the town of Gosport to the city of Portsmouth and vice versa.

Nowadays, the crossing is comfortable, but that was not always the case. In days gone by the travellers were tough, braving open decks in all weathers. Today, however, there is plenty of accommodation in lounges and viewing decks. The ferries are able to deal with disabled people and those of us that are older can now travel in comfort. There is even a discount for pensioners, on tickets used after peak travelling times, so it never comes as a surprise to see groups of pensioners congregating either on the pontoon or in the gardens on the Gosport side, awaiting that magic time when they can travel for less.

Unlike the bus pass scheme, however, it is not free to pensioners at any time. At the time of writing, the ferry service is owned by a private company called FIH, which is short for Falkland Island Holdings, and it needs to make a profit. Whilst it is a short journey across the water, costs are high, and falling passenger numbers have resulted in a need for almost an annual increase. Should a person or couple need to cross regularly, it can become a burden financially and in particular, to those groups of people with a fixed income.

This novel follows on from my previous book, 'Going Over the Water' about the history of the Gosport Ferry as told by lots of people of Gosport.

David Gary
September 2020

CHAPTER 1

The girl could have been no more than twenty, and she wore a pair of shorts that left very little to the imagination regarding her rear. Hardy could not take his eyes off her, especially when she went up for Communion and knelt at the altar. It did have its plus points coming to church, he thought. Joyce, his wife, was thinking something quite different and was irritated by Hardy appearing to worship something other than the God they were meant to be worshiping in this place.

There were about twenty at the most in the congregation. The singing had been painful – it always seemed to be, despite the volume coming from the six people in the choir. The congregation was lucky in some respects inasmuch as they still had an organist, albeit limited by his repertoire of some twelve hymns. *Praise my Soul the King of Heaven* was well-practised now by everyone, and his rendition of *Holy Holy Holy* was considered by some in the congregation to have lost its impact.

Joyce told herself she really had to face reality; these Sunday morning services were getting to the point whereby the majority of the congregation might just as well remain in church to save money on transporting them back there for their own funerals. It was probably, she thought, the same in every church up and down the country.

At long last they were approaching the end of the service. She had done her bit, she had said 'hello' to her God and praised him: surely she would get inside the gates when she had suffered every Sunday like this. Today the church was cool, and at that time of the year a blessed relief from the hot weather outside, but of course in winter it was quite the opposite. The old building had never been designed for comfort and the central heating system was totally inadequate to heat the place on a Sunday in January. In common with many church buildings, this one suffered from the ability to swallow money in large quantities, so the heating system was run on a miserly level. Joyce could not remember a time when there was not an appeal taking place to raise cash for some currently failing fabric of the building.

"Go in peace, and serve the Lord," the vicar announced in his clipped English accent. This appeal signalled they were near to the end of the service, an end to the numb backsides, and the pins and needles in the legs. Soon they would be able to move and walk; a blessed relief, she always thought, for those now seized-up joints crying out for some lubrication. He was a portly vicar, ex-Services like most around the Gosport and Portsmouth area were. His hair was jet black, and in an old-fashioned way, thought Joyce, he still relied on some form of hair grease to keep it swept backwards, firmly following the shape of the skull. If Joyce had anything to do with him, she would place him on a diet and insist that he gave himself a good scrub. In her eyes the vicar always looked grubby and this was backed by a sort of stale aroma that surrounded him.

"In the name of Christ, Amen," was the response from the congregation.

"Now let us put an arm around the people that surround us in a show of unity and love." The vicar was enthusiastic on this issue. The church is, after all, about 'love' he would proffer.

At this point, however, Joyce reached the limit of her Christianity as preached and understood by this vicar. She did not like this sort of touchy feely stuff that had worked its way into some Church of England services. We are not like this, she thought - we have always been reserved and frankly that was the way she liked it. Not in her seventy years had she ever hugged a stranger she had not even spoken to, and no way was she about to start. She was certainly not hugging her husband Hardy, who was of course standing next to her.

Not unusually, she had had enough of him that particular Sunday morning with his constant moaning that bits of his body didn't work any more, and his constant visits to the toilet. In fact, she thought, their life was now governed by the toilet. He knew of every toilet in the town, he knew where service stations were on the M3, and for all she knew he had probably obtained a map of toilets all over the country, or even Europe.

She had told him to either go to the doctor about it or shut up. That was her view. She had told him so many times, each occasion sparking yet another row, because Hardy saw it as another attack by her upon his manhood. He believed she would often be thinking "Where was the man I married?" He even wondered that himself sometimes.

The outing to the church service had followed another humiliating tirade from Joyce regarding the whereabouts of his cufflinks. Even Hardy had no expectation that she would ever turn to him for a hug, albeit in the name of Christ. Hardy imagined that Joyce was in cahoots with Christ and had obtained an exemption clause in her contract with him. This meant she was able to leave Hardy out of any love and affection. Instead, she turned to the elderly little round guy to her right. He stood with the aid of a walking stick. She knew him quite well: his name was Bert. She gently put her arm around his shoulder, and he turned to her and awkwardly put his hand on her shoulder. It lasted seconds. But it was long enough, as there had been a waft of something quite stale coming from Bert's suit. This agonising duty had been completed by Joyce; she had given into peer pressure, and whilst her actions could only be marginally described as a hug, it was more than sufficient in her mind. Meanwhile, Hardy had turned to his left and found nobody, so no need for any 'activity' there.

The 'old' were differentiated by both their demeanour and their dress. The few of the younger generations that had turned up seemed not to dress for church, pitching up in jeans, T-shirts and even shorts, a trend that both Joyce and Hardy, unusually for them, found common ground in disliking. "But if you want 'the young' to attend anything these days, it has to be done on their terms," the vicar had explained a few months ago when the subject had come up in conversation.

So the one pew occupied by a group of twenty-somethings had to be tolerated and their excessive hugging equally so. They were at the other side of the church, both figuratively and in reality. Joyce would smile at them. The young ones wanted to be inclusive – age should mean nothing, they would argue, and so they would smile back in that condescending manner attributed to 'do gooders' worldwide these days. It would tick one of their boxes, Joyce supposed, showing some care and respect for 'the elderly'. Joyce did not actually want much to do with that.

She would tolerate them, and that would be it. The vicar had indeed once pointed out to her: "Of course you realise those jeans with the cuts in them probable cost three times as much as an ordinary pair of trousers?"

The final hymn demanded some sort of forgiveness: "Dear Lord and father of mankind, forgive our foolish ways." Joyce was still a long way off of forgiving anyone their foolish ways. In fact she gave foolish people little house-room. The service came to an end. There would be the normal chat between other members of the congregation, and the vicar would always be at the door to bid farewell or make sure you left. Joyce was never quite sure which, particularly after two allegedly homeless men had been found sheltering in the church a few months back. The Parochial Church Council had been outraged. What damage had these 'homeless' caused? She had parted company with the vicar on this one as well, in as much as he had been suggesting that the role of the church may indeed include the duty to provide shelter for homeless people, particularly in bad weather. Joyce had insisted that this was a political matter and was quite properly the remit of the Government of the day.

They filed out into the aisle.

"See you on Tuesday then, Bert," she reminded him as he walked off in a laboured manner.

"Oh yes, I'll be there for sure." He turned to reassure her. He winced as he did so, and she was aware that the poor man must be in some sort of pain.

Tuesday 3rd August dawned a gorgeous day with a cloudless sky, a big blue sky, with the temperature well into the teens even early in the morning. Apart from the lovely weather, it was not an unusual day. A scattering of people could be seen sitting along the sea front, staring into the busy Portsmouth Harbour. The sea was still, sporting a rich green colour, which turned into the traditional azure as one's vision was drawn out into Spithead. The Spinnaker Tower gleamed in the sunlight. Also gleaming, some monied person had parked his or her ostentatious yacht onto the mornings in front of the tower adding a sense of wealth to the scene.

Two elderly Jehovah's Witnesses were standing with their stand of books, the books that posed eye-watering questions like 'Who is God?' The Witnesses always parked themselves at the top of the ferry pontoon hoping, usually in vain, for just one bite from what seemed to them to be an unconcerned public. They were desperate to explain to just one soul the joys of their religion. The Witnesses were engaged in conversation with each other, but then they always are. Day in day out they stood there, regardless of the weather. God should surely reward them.

The ticket office for the Gosport Ferry was never actually devoid of staff, but never that busy either. Lots of older people could remember queues trailing back for yards, and you would stand there watching the ferry leave the pontoon whilst still waiting for your ticket. The fact that the office was nearly always staffed provided a welcome reassurance for many pensioners, able to speak for once to a human being instead of the now increasingly familiar electronic voice. Of course the ferry company had succumbed to the craze for ticket-dispensing machines, totally so on the Portsmouth side, and a machine was also provided on the Gosport side. Many customers would be sad when the ticket office went, as it surely would. Lots of people were not looking forward to following the instructions of an electronic voice.

A big purple single-deck bus was running its engine, stationary in its bay at the bus station adjacent to the ferry terminal, polluting nicely the previously relatively clean sea air that wafted in from the Solent and Spithead. The bus was readying itself for the regular trip to Fareham It was into this scene of 'normality' that the 'group' was to meet.

Olly had alighted from that big purple bus and was first to arrive. He was always first to arrive, anywhere. He always enjoyed gazing out onto the scene that greeted people alighting from the buses. Olly gazed out into the harbour and across to the new Gunwharf Quays shopping outlet, so different he thought to the days when that area was HMS VERNON, the minesweeper base. He remembered back in 1976 HRH Prince Charles, as a skipper, brought in his minesweeper HMS Bronington into and out of the base almost on a daily basis. He had recently read that the ship (or boat, as minesweepers are known), was now in Birkenhead, semi-sunk with its stern on the bottom. A typical example of the ravages of time.

Olly stared out at the harbour, remembering that crazy planning meeting back in a cooler May, when he had met with Bert, Joyce and Hardy. Now, now the actual day was here, he frankly wondered why he had not put a stop to it back then, but he hadn't and he was now committed. He never went back on commitment.

Olly's tall thin frame projected his now-thinning greying black-haired head above that of most other people. He wore spectacles with black frames. He held himself upright - he had not succumbed to any bent-over look yet but his stance also gave him an air of authority. He was blessed with many talents, but dress sense was not one of them. His wife had despaired of telling him that his size eleven 'wide' Clark's shoes were inappropriate for jeans that tapered in as the leg got closer to the foot, and the fact that his foot was so far from his waist made it seem even more bizarre. But they were comfortable, he would argue, and as he had got older he had become even less concerned about appearance. Perhaps one gets less vain as one gets older, he thought.

He looked around and spotted Joyce and Hardy making their way across the road that separated the town from the seafront. He felt a small sense of relief that at least they were here, even though the thought of being bossed around yet again by Joyce filled him with dread. He sometimes made a stand against her, only to be rolled into the ground, and unless he turned things ugly he would just have to bite his tongue today and put up with it. He noticed that Hardy walked a bit funnily these days; it wasn't really a limp, more of an imperfection that made him list slightly to starboard.

"Morning to you both," he boomed. Confidence was never visibly lacking with Olly, even though in private he often suffered from many insecurities, but it never appeared that way in public. In fact he often over-compensated and people misread that as aggression. He used his arms and hands expressively, waving them around like a windmill, which was not really surprising given that his family had originated many years ago in southern France. The French were renowned for expressive arm and hand movements.

"Mmmm, I hope so. I hope it's a very good morning, that's all I can say."

Hardy always took a long time to deliver any response or message; his Suffolk drawl went slowly and no one would want to rely on him to inform an ambulance crew that someone appeared to be having a heart attack. Joyce made up for that, however, and fed up with his pessimism, curtly told Hardy not to be such a 'wimp'.

"I always get this, every time something in life is slightly different, this is what I get. You've no idea, Olly, how boring and demoralising he can be." She was earnest.

Olly did have a rough idea but even so, he knew not to agree with her because she could just as easily suddenly change sides and close ranks around her husband, as if you had become the aggressor and not her, despite her remarks. So he ignored her, choosing to look around at the scenery.

Joyce, however, was in many ways the female equivalent of Olly; she too was very upright, making her taller than most females, and her presumably dyed blonde hair was done in a style that also increased her height by about an inch. She was not fat, but not thin either, though unlike Olly, she was fashion conscious and dressed smartly. Even today, she sported heels on her shoes that gave her even more height. She never skimped on make-up and made sure people knew her clothing was top-end, right the way down to her underwear. Unusually for a woman of her age, she often boasted she could wear 'sexy' gear, her figure not having been ruined, she claimed, by the carrying of a child. She too was spectacled, but these were 'classy' spectacles, out of reach for those who attended cheaper shops.

The day was sunny and now getting really warm, and the sea as flat as a millpond. It gave off an odour that flooded the nostrils and made one feel alive. One of the Gosport ferries had just berthed, its side thrusters throwing a foaming white stream into the harbour, keeping her safely up against the pontoon despite the rocking from the wake of a large outgoing cross-Channel ferry. There was a yacht making its way out in the small boats channel, maybe for a day's sailing in the Solent, and the Isle of Wight car ferry was edging its way out backwards, transporting vehicles over to the island. It was sounding its warning notice to the passengers, either that or a car alarm was going off in the hold. A Ministry of Defence police patrol launch made its way over to some hapless rower, an easy target for them to shout at, but Olly thought they were right to do so in these times of not knowing what people were doing. The police manning boats needed to avoid the 'blame culture' if correct procedures had not been followed. These days there was a fifty-metre exclusion zone around all Royal Navy warships, and the rower was probably infringing that.

The 'group' was not yet fully formed. It was still too early to use a pensioner ticket on the ferry, and of course one or two of the others would still be waiting to use their bus pass that also did not start until half past nine. No way were such people prepared to actually pay a bus fare when they could travel for free just five minutes later.

"I say Hardy, nice to see you. I'm so nervous about today, the whole thing you know, it could go so terribly wrong and all of us end up as criminals." Bert had appeared as if from nowhere, the same short round little figure, previously having been hugged in church slightly bent over, using a walking stick. He was wearing a suit and tie, even today in this warmth. His face was slightly flushed with the mounting heat and the frustrations that he always had within him, or was it the brandy from last night? He was not clean-shaven but it was not 'designer stubble', more a case of not being quite able to see in his bathroom mirror, consequently he missed large parts down the sides of his face. He carried a rolled-up banner under his free arm, and it was obviously giving him problems, being heavier than it looked.

Bert's anxiety stemmed from what they were about to do. The anxiety was also felt by Hardy who had appointed himself as the man in charge. Joyce had also supported his leadership, just providing he did what she 'suggested'.

What had seemed like a fantastic idea fuelled by sherry in the traditional get-together after church now seemed less so. The group had become activists in the name of greater recognition for matters that affected the elderly. Something astounding needed to be done, they had said, like hijacking the Gosport Ferry and sailing it to France. Over there they imagined being joined by the 'yellow vests', and a massive movement could take place all over Europe, changing attitudes towards elderly people.

Bert's frustration this time had been set off yet again by having to pay for a ferry ticket. He and others felt so very strongly that the ferry should be part of the bus pass scheme, with free passage for pensioners after nine-thirty.

"Ah, hello Bert." Hardy was pleased to see him, but seldom would one recognise such emotions in Hardy. Hardy's speech never speeded or slowed, never raised its tone nor lowered, except of course when dealing with his wife. In fact, Hardy could make 'hello' seem really boring. Hardy's facial expressions were also difficult to read – again, like his voice, never really changing from a pained look that seemed to be permanent. Hardy was of medium height, but felt short because Joyce was above average for a woman.

He was heavy, not fat, but on the heavy side with the inevitable male belly. Unfair, he thought, because he hardly ever drank beer, staying mainly with spirits or wine. He looked his age of seventy-two even though he still had hair; his face was lined and weathered. His hair was always neatly combed in a very conventional manner.

Bert was eighty-one. He was single - he had been a bachelor all of his life. His short time in the army as a National Serviceman had opened his eyes to life, but they had quickly closed again when he returned to his parents' home and his job in the Housing Department of the local council. He had never considered himself anything other than a clerk in the Housing Department, counting out the rent money and balancing it. He had done it for thirty-odd years and he had seen many changes in that time. It had not been the sort of job his parents had in mind for him. His father had had a distinguished military career with the Royal Navy, and his son's lack of enthusiasm to continue the family tradition had not pleased him. So there had always been an underlying tension in the home, and to some degree when his parents had died there was a release of that constant nag that he had failed his father's expectations.

Bert had, however, over the years, become increasingly angry and bitter, unable to find a release for the many things he now did not approve of. The social changes that had occurred under various governments, whilst somewhat justified, had in his opinion gone too far in supporting the lazy, feckless and morally corrupt. Indeed, he found himself in trouble with his employer, the local council, for expressing his views in a quite forthright way to a young family pleading poverty and not paying their rent, when he had seen them out smoking and drinking cans of lager just three days earlier. He was at a loss as to why the council had not backed him and had given the impression of supporting the lifestyle of these 'indolent inadequates' over him. The family needed telling as to where they were going wrong. He had seen it every week, how young girls who irresponsibly got pregnant could get a house and then not even bother to pay the rent. Their homes were ill kept. They seem to think that if you threw an empty baked bean can into the garden, a new baked bean tree would grow from it.

Bert's job had fed his moods and attitudes, through his exposure to people who would be considered 'vulnerable'.

But now he was retired, television journalists and the Daily Mail stoked and reinforced his anger. There seemed to be a transfer of responsibility from the individual to anyone other than themselves. He would argue that instead of catching terrorists, all innocent and normal people had to suffer in airports, being searched, unpacking one's medication and having to practically undress to go through those confounded machines. If your car was broken into and stuff stolen, it was the victim's fault because you left something on full view on the back seat. How wrong was that, he would argue? Now, he felt, in some way this was his chance to strike back, to make a statement that the good people in the world deserved some consideration as well.

Hardy, on the other hand, just felt angry. If he really thought about it, the reasons seemed numerous, but probably deep down it revolved around the relationship with his wife and what he saw as her constant oppression. Joyce dominated his life - she arranged everything, she told him where to be, when, when he could pick his nose, who he could befriend, who he had to dislike and how fast or slow to drive. She would tell him that he had missed the last right turn, and blame him for not knowing where he was going, even though he could not remember for the life of him ever being told where they were headed. But he did know about today and he had a role to play, and he harboured a remote hope that she might, just might, see him in a different light.

Today, she had so far limited herself to checking if he had used the toilet before leaving home, but she had then complained to him about the fact that it was necessary to remind him. It was a tradition that was upheld daily whenever they were going out. Women had always checked with him whether he needed the toilet before he went out, right from being a child when his mother had made him use the toilet whether he wanted to or not. Now it was the duty of his wife and when asked, he invariably decided that it would be a 'good idea', and the urge would come, and there was never a problem, and everyone was happy.

He, however, had a problem with his anger, a deep-seated anger that was probably directed as much at himself as her. He should have taken charge years ago, put her in her place instead of just putting up with things for a quiet life. Their marriage had become a habit years ago more than a relationship. But then many things in life are like that, he thought. At least he had the company of a woman and had known the sensual delights of her female body over the years, the arms that comforted him during distress and made things alright. That, he thought, as he stood there gazing at Bert was much more than that poor man had experienced.

So, they stood waiting for the others to join them. Over by the ferry office, Olly was doing some sort of war dance, waving his arms around in the air, directed at some unfortunate man he had cornered up against the wall. Being a tremendously clear-thinking man, debating with Olly was difficult. When cornered by him, it was not always a pleasant experience. His view on many things was based on logic, and as he had been told in his previous workplace, logic could not always be applied to human emotions. That was his weakness, but to be fair to him he tried really hard to understand. His wife had often said that it was so difficult for him - it was like asking a man to imagine giving birth.

"Who's the unlucky man Olly's cornered?" asked Bert.

"Isn't it that councillor chap, what's his name?"

"Cripps."

"No, it's not him. It's on the tip of my tongue, oh bloody hell what is it?"

"It's that one that came to give us a talk, isn't it?" Joyce added constructively.

"No it's not, it wasn't him, he's the one who chaired that meeting the other night."

"What meeting?" asked Joyce. "I never went to a meeting, if there was a meeting, I should have gone." Hardy rolled his eyes. A meeting without Joyce, good grief!

"You don't have to be at every meeting, Joyce." A brave remark from Hardy.

There was no response from Joyce. Well, none perceptible to Bert. But Hardy, a husband of many years' experience, did pick up a response that withered him, that turned him again into a gibbering heap. The response was in the air, it was on her face, in fact it was all around him, and he did what he was now best at doing, he shut up.

So nobody could actually establish who Olly was haranguing. Like lots of conversations these days, the conversation died, firstly because it had gone off the subject and secondly because the memory was not quite what it used to be, and thirdly because Hardy had shut up, obeying those unheard spiritually transmitted instructions from 'her'.

It was ten minutes later, when the pensioner bus pass could be used, that Ken and Kenneth turned up, along with a lady who was with …well to be frank, it seemed both Ken and Kenneth. The three of them always travelled and ate together and seemed to come as a package of three. Such behaviour inevitably led to gossip and wild speculation from some of the more furtive minds in their social circle. The group always found it difficult to deal with two men of the same name, so one they called Ken and the other Kenneth.

Sarah was the woman with Kenneth and Ken: officially she was with Ken. They had become great friends, so much so that their lives had merged into one homogenous blob, whereby they were indistinguishable as anything other than a threesome.

Sarah was a well-educated woman, yet doubted herself. No one was absolutely certain about her dark red hair. Was it a wig? The consensus was 'no' because it was always there but in different forms of arrangement, or disarrangement as the case may be. Joyce always gave her the benefit of the doubt, yet it had been Joyce that had cast doubt in the first place.

Joyce of course was hugely sceptical about the three of them. She actually did know which of the Kens that Sarah was an 'item' with. But to people who did not know them, Joyce took great pleasure in suggesting a three-way relationship that would raise eyebrows in normal company. Hardy wondered whether the three of them actually played to Joyce. Sarah seemed sometimes to aid Joyce's suspicions doing things like calling both of the Kens 'darling', she called both of them 'love', and of course she called both of them Ken. How, Joyce wondered, did either of the Kens know when she was talking to him? If Sarah did call one Ken and the other Kenneth, did that correspond to the understanding by the group of who was Ken and who was Kenneth?

For Hardy, it was a relief that the two Kens had turned up, along with Sarah. Hardy ticked off his list: all were present now. In fact Ken took it too far by even reporting "all present and correct sir."

Ken was big; he was overweight and needed a walking stick. He was slow in his walking, whilst Kenneth was OK, not fat, not thin, not fast but not slow either, and he was essential to their aim because of his ability to get things done quietly and without fuss. Olly would also get things done but created so much fuss which often created a sense of anxiety, affecting those involved.

· "So, we're ready then. Olly … Olly." Hardy summoned Olly to the group, because Olly was still engaged with the man whose name had escaped everyone.

"Now, has everyone got tickets?"

It was a rhetorical question really, because nobody actually answered.

"OK, I think we are ready then."

A panicky voice piped up.

"Hardy, Hardy, my God, did you bring your pills?"

"Oh for pity's sake Joyce, course I did … didn't I?" His voice trailed off.

"Well, I haven't got them," she answered curtly with the emphasis on 'I'.

"There's always some in your handbag."

"I'm telling you Hardy, I've not got any of your pills in this bag. Yes, I've got some in my blue bag but not in this grey one." She laboured each word.

"Oh, of course, I should have thought about that shouldn't I? Change your handbag and my bloody life changes too."

"You haven't got them, have you?" Joyce was eager to get to the bottom line.

"Doesn't look like it. I can't live without them, I have to have them, I really need them."

"Of course you do – you will be useless without them."

There was a collective sigh from the others.

"Look," said Olly, "You're patently are not going to last many hours in a fit state without them, and standing around here talking is just wasting time. I suggest the rest of us go off to the cafe, get a coffee or something, whilst you go off and get them."

"Oh great, this is a good start, a really good start. We will have to delay the whole operation while Hardy goes off to get his pills." said a Ken in his best offended voice.

"Guess that's about the state of it," added Olly. "So let's make the decision then; the operation is delayed for one hour while Hardy gets his pills."

"Well, I hope you are proud of yourself," Joyce said in such a manner that everyone knew it was, shall we say, at the very minimum edged with sarcasm.

Hardy departed for the bus, feeling humiliated again and with some good reason really.

The others went over to the cafe. "Neutral talk everyone, understand? Neutral. Nothing about today at all, got it?"

Nobody answered again but Olly was sure everyone had got it.

"We'll share a cup, shall we, Ken?" He was given no time to answer before Sarah addressed the rest of the group. "If Ken has a whole mug of coffee, it goes straight through him these days, he'll spend most of the time in the toilet."

"Oh thanks for sharing that information with everyone, Sarah."

"Yes, I know darling, but it is true though, isn't it?"

The excitement was officially delayed for one hour.

CHAPTER 2

Olly

With the departure of Hardy to collect his pills, Olly now had a short time to reflect. He sat there in the cafe musing over lots of things, but mainly examining why he was there at all. He drifted off into a world of his own, away from the madness that seemed to surround him. He went back to those days of his past.

Olly had worked in the IT industry. He had seen the industry bloom from the early days of punch-card girls, sitting punching holes into reels of tape, miles of them, each hole representing information, right up to some six years ago when he had retired from work. The world was now largely dependant on IT. He had realised many years ago that this was a rapidly changing industry, bringing many changes to people's lives. In fact, he argued, this would be seen as a second industrial revolution in years to come. He had always told his staff, albeit in a light-hearted manner, that if they took a fortnight off work, there was a good chance that when they came back to work they might very well be de-skilled. It had to be said, however, that such advice seldom persuaded anyone to avoid taking leave, and a quick read of magazines would bring them back up to date.

On reflection, it seemed crazy that a machine that once took up a whole room, and sometimes more, was now contained in a seven by seven-inch thin case. He remembered many years ago now, arguing … no perhaps the word was 'debating' … with some of his staff about the 'need' for cash dispensing machines in the wall of banks. "Why do you need them when you can just go in the bank and get cash?" was the quite reasonable response. His argument was that cash would be available twenty-four hours a day, seven days a week. Even his own staff had not got it back then. Who needs cash in the middle of the night, they would argue? But now he took pride in the fact that he was right and that cash dispensers up and down the country were in everyday use by pretty much the whole population.

In fact, things had gone full circle and cash machines might be under threat as the product they dispensed, actual cash, wa rapidly becoming old fashioned. He had been told on one of his recent visits to London, when buying drinks with cash, that he wouldn't be able to do that for much longer.

"How stupid is that?" Olly had argued, never leaving anything unchallenged. "You should tell your managers, one blip with your systems, one hour power cut, and you are out of business. Cash is accepted and it is reliable, it is part of our DNA. And I would have thought you younger people should be concerned that if you lose cash, every transaction you make will be traceable. In fact do you know that two thirds of American paper dollars are actually held outside the country?" He queried himself – what did that have to do with it?

"I guess that means crime would collapse then – any money obtained from criminal activity would be traceable."

The young man behind the bar had entered the debate

with gusto, and to Olly had given him credit for what was a good point. But Olly could still not see any government in the near future having the 'balls' to scrap cash.

Was that a yesteryear opinion? The cash issue would surely expose the gulf between the 'know how to do it' brigade, and those that didn't. Again, it would probably be a further divisive issue in society and as sure as eggs were eggs, it would manifest itself along ageist lines. He reasoned that the lack of paper notes would also be an issue for those snorting cocaine.

By his own philosophy, being out of the hot-house of development for some six years meant that he was in effect now de-skilled himself and he felt to a degree, useless. He had become more aware of his vulnerabilities, often re-enforced by society, based on his appearance, that of an ageing man. There had been a young man in his Building Society who talked to him like he was a five-year-old child. The man had assumed Olly was not quite able to understand how to, or the need to 'sign in' when looking at his account 'on line'.

"And of course you mustn't tell anyone your passwords," the man had added earnestly.

Olly had just agreed, nodding in a nonchalant manner, giving in and ostensibly playing the part of the stupid pensioner. He just did not want the hassle of making the point that it had been him and his ilk that had actually thought of passwords in the first place, many years ago.

His work had meant a lot to him. He had been lucky; he had worked in a happy environment along with people that he had largely understood and got on with. But towards the end there had been an increasing tension between him and the 'up and comings.' He baulked at modern management methods that were finding their way into his previously content and happy world. He admitted he was not good with people, few in the IT industry were, he would reason. He had found it difficult to interject himself into matters where he felt he had no place being, yet, according to those 'that matter', in order to get the best out of people it was sometimes necessary to intervene when behaviour by one or two people was a threat to a happy workforce. Those with MBAs would tell him that as a manager he was not just responsible for delivering IT, but indeed all the 'works of God'.

Because he didn't look or listen to what he called gossip, he had become somewhat isolated from the activities of his staff. He had not noticed, for example, the affair between one of his married male members of staff and a married woman in another department. Like many people, he assumed his standards were also those of others. Olly's standards were in fact extremely moral, holding onto what could be called Christian ethics.

Apparently, so he had been confidentially told later, the 'affair' was the talk of the whole building. Olly had not noticed the long lunch breaks, the working late that corresponded with the working late of the other party. No, he had later told his confidant, his staff member had not come to his attention because he was entitled to long lunch breaks, and he made up the time, and he did his job – what else could one ask for?

"Olly, they came back from lunch reeking of sex, everyone knew," he had been told. Olly had been bewildered for two reasons: firstly, how do you smell sex? And again he had asked what on earth it had to do with him as long as his employee did his job?

"It's not what's happening in the moment, today, Olly. It's the fallout when the shit hits the fan. Look, it's inevitable that we were going to have two wrecks in the organisation. They already spend lots of their time covering for each other, pretending to everyone that nothing is happening. It can't go on like this; one of them is pretty sure to leave their wife or husband, and then what happens?"

So what was he meant to do about it?

"Point out that his employee is the 'talk of the building', point out that this could ruin his marriage, point out that it could ruin both of their lives, point out that if performance suffered as a consequence of what they were up to the organisation would have to take a view of their continued association." Olly's advisor had almost pleaded.

"No, no, no," Olly had said, this wasn't what he did, he solved IT issues, he made sure that the payment made by a member of the public appeared in the bank balance and could be traced. He told the gardens department when to plant bulbs and wallflowers, he designed screens that showed budgets and could transmit committee reports to people's homes in seconds.

Never did he deal with affairs of the heart, in fact he had never been sure that he even understood such things, and as for this sex stuff, he just didn't want to even bring the subject up, let alone give any advice.

But his department had been rocked by the affair and, using the sort of language the Sun would use, staff were 'reeling' from the implications. It did indeed disrupt work as it became more and more public, and of course the inevitable had happened. The woman involved took matters more seriously than the man, and made the decision that she could no longer deceive her husband and that a clean break would now be in order.

She was confident that her lover in Olly's IT department would join her and a new life would be just over the horizon. It was, of course, more messy than that. He had children and was less than keen to break his family up. She pressured him to leave his wife and both parties started showing signs of stress in the office. Both him and his lover then took to drink. They would drink wine to start with and then it moved to vodka. There were massive mood changes from both of them, upsetting for all around, and long absences from work occurred, leading to wild speculation amongst staff and management alike. Staff were taking sides, but Olly had refused to comment, let alone get involved. She became increasingly 'sick' and people were getting upset at having to cover her when they knew full well what the 'sicky' was. The 'sicky' was usually a hangover, and 'management' seem to be doing nothing about it. So, and this is the bit he didn't like, it was he, Olly, that was perceived to be lacking – it was he that was 'interviewed' by the new Personnel people.

A bloody enquiry. An enquiry as to what he, yes, he Olly, could have done to prevent the kerfuffle.

They were very polite, very formal, and spent most of their time ticking boxes. Brian, the Chief Personnel Officer, always carried a look of angst. That caring sincere look that was his profession's trademark, much like social workers constantly wore. The enquiry went right into the morale in Olly's IT department. What did he do to team build? Olly had a job connecting that question to the 'affair'. Apparently the personnel officer's concern was the loss of manpower due to sickness and he asked Olly to do a 'welcome back' interview whenever his employee did show his face.

The 'welcome back' interview had been introduced about a year before these events, and to be fair had been met with some scepticism by senior managers including Olly. Olly took the view that such an interview undermined the trust that a manager should show his staff. The idea was to speak to any member of staff, not in an adversarial way but in a constructive manner, seeing whether there were long-term issues, or anything that the organisation could do to help avoid further bouts of sickness. It had, despite the skepticism, been quite effective, particularly weeding out the Friday sickness, or better known as the 'night after skittles sickness'. It did also help the organisation deal with very sad or serious cases of sickness in a much more sympathetic way, and amongst staff the scheme had slowly gained ground as being a sign that their employer may actually 'care'.

For Olly the 'Enquiry' had been a personal thing. Personnel as a department had all been nice enough and never pointed any finger. Quite the contrary in fact; they realised that there was probably a training need in the organisation as a whole, and the issue could be completely turned around onto them. So the foot on the throttle of vengeance was lifted.

Olly felt that the Personnel Officer did retain a sense of respect for him as someone that had given loyal service for many years and had generally served the organisation well, which pleased him, and made him feel good for a little while. There was to be no official fall-out, but it was recommended that Olly attend various courses connected to managing people.

The real damage, however, was at that moment slightly hidden to others. Olly's head had been got at. It had been quite an overwhelming event for him. It was not the first time, of course, that he had been challenged about his managerial skills, but this was one that he had not seen coming. Even when pointed out to him, kindly and sympathetically by colleagues he now regarded as friends, that he had still not addressed his management style, he became even more depressed. He had done nothing because basically he felt either out of his depth or could not justify any actions in getting involved in these people's lives. They were, after all, the same as all of us, he felt, two pieces of flesh doing their best to navigate life's often lonely trail.

The event changed his relationship with his work environment. That in turn affected his moods at home, and work became over time increasingly more difficult for him to cope with and much less pleasant. It also had not been helped by the resignation of the said adulterer. The man would be difficult to replace having been a very dependable programmer.

A loud crash in the cafe's kitchen brought Olly back to his surroundings. Someone had obviously dropped some plates, which hopefully he thought would at least save them washing up, but then for these people he assumed profit margins were poor, trying to compete with the bigger chains like Greggs just over the road: broken plates equalled more costs. Olly stood immediately, enquiring if he could do anything to help. "One of those things, mate," he was told, "but thanks anyway." Olly gave his usual Gaelic shrug, one of the many gestures he used to convey his thoughts. The rest of his group seemed little concerned.

Olly was expressive and direct. He was well known for waving his hands about. His French ancestors, from whom without doubt he had inherited the habit, were something he was quite proud of. It made him slightly more interesting, but the hand and arm waving had sometimes got him into trouble. It had been embarrassing when, with his boss and one other colleague, on a crowded train going into Paddington one morning for a meeting, he had been explaining the pros and cons of his favourite project. It was a good project no doubt, and had been labelled 'Tell us once'.

"Imagine," he begged his rather captive audience, "one telephone call, one email to just one person in the authority, and every action required is taken because we link systems."

At this point Olly was in what some called 'missionary mode'.

As always, the train filled at Reading, so the seat next to him was now occupied by a poor unsuspecting passenger. Olly did not stop his debate with his colleagues sitting opposite him, and as his argument proceeded to its point, its high point, his arms spread like an eagle taking off from its perch, knocking the poor man's coffee clean out of his grasp and sending it flying across the carriage. The point of Olly's argument was largely lost in the turmoil that followed, with at least five other passengers now having to sponge the gentle aroma of coffee from their splattered clothes, even outperforming the aroma of Chanel. A mad search ensued for tissues, for serviettes and any other item that provided a mopping-up ability.

A further incident that had led to him believing that there was a 'sell by' date printed on it had been caused by the unlikely event of a visitor from an Eastern Bloc county, who attended on his friend and colleague, the man responsible for revenue. Olly could not ever remember the guy's name, unpronounceable as it was. All he could remember was that the gentleman had the deepest voice he had ever heard, was large and bald, and no doubt carried a bottle of vodka in the true tradition of men from that region of the world. For some reason, this guy had become friends with the local Rent Officer, who thought it would be a good idea for him to learn about the way the UK administered taxes, the said Eastern Bloc man being a 'high' official in the Treasury of his country. Olly had been invited to the meeting to talk about the joined-up policy that the council was pursuing through the use of IT.

"So," said the Eastern Bloc gentleman, "You collect the taxes that runs the hospital and things."

"Ah, no, we collect the Council tax. Hospitals are run by general taxation."

"General Taxation?"

"Yes, Income Tax, a tax on income."

"I see, so council tax pays for shall we say the roads?"

"Ah no, we pay a road fund licence for that - each car is taxed."

"So, what about water supplies and drainage?"

"Well, er um, we pay separate bills for that, one to the water board and another to the authority responsible for drainage, and rivers and things."

By this time the man from the Eastern Bloc was looking confused.

"Education then?"

"Yes, yes, the council tax does contribute towards that, but education is responsibility of the County Council, who precept upon us."

"What about the BBC? We are envious of the BBC in our country?"

"Oh no, that is a separate tax called a licence."

"Pensions?"

"No, that is paid for out of contributions to the National

Insurance scheme."

By now, the man from the Eastern Bloc was looking totally bewildered, and by now Olly had had a question of his own, directed at the man from the Eastern Bloc country.

"Can I ask how many different taxes you have?"

"We have one that pays for everything. People must pay what is demanded by the state."

"You have one tax and you want to study us?"

"Yes, because we sometime have problems getting people to pay, so I wanted to know how you collect your tax, and if you say to them how their money is being used."

"Oh yes, we do that, but we have to go to court if they don't pay, and often the court will make an arrangement with them. What do you do?"

"Oh sometimes we shoot them, then everyone else pays."

Olly was astounded; he was lost for words, which for Olly was rare indeed.

The man from the Eastern Bloc added quickly, "But we need to change that in order to get into the EU. The EU does not like that collection method.'

"I should think you do need to change." Olly was exploding internally with this perceived injustice of shooting people for not paying taxes, and those in the room who knew him recognised the signs. Before Olly kicked off big-time, his friend ushered him out of the room, surely avoiding a diplomatic incident. But Olly had not let it rest, writing later to his MP and causing all sorts of bad feelings which had not endeared him to 'those that matter.' He just did not get the fact that the man had been joking. But then he had always found jokes difficult.

There was an opportunity coming to put his hand up for early retirement, and whilst a year previously he would not of given it any thought, now things were different. His wife was keen for him to get out. She had noticed the changes in his moods, in his keenness to go off to work on a Monday morning. The tell-tale signs were there, that much longer in this environment would lead to a full scale breakdown or some other catastrophe, and that was not worth it when there was an exit strategy available.

Olly was a family man: he had two sons, one doing very well for himself and the other on the 'just managing' scale. Despite Olly's peculiarities, the boys experienced a very normal childhood. Olly's job had allowed his wife to stay at home, and do the traditional homemaker chores and responsibilities. However, this had had mixed blessings, leaving her feeling somewhat isolated, and when the time did come that she could go out to work and contribute to the family cash, she found it very difficult. Olly failed to understand this and it created tension between them. Olly brought into his personal life the same lack of attributes that he brought to his professional life: his failure to understand emotions that he considered to be illogical. Olly's idea of counselling was to ask the individual if he or she understood that they were wrong to feel the way they did. That approach had failed both at work and in his private life and had created a bit of a crisis in their marriage, which to his knowledge had never occurred before. It did concern and he supposed upset him that his wife was finding life difficult. There was just no way he could understand it because no logic could be applied. He didn't like to see her like this, but what could he do?

It took his wife's mother to explain and to intervene, and the intervention probably avoided a relationship breakdown. In some ways she made them both understand each other a little better, and had suggested that Olly might even be on the spectrum of autism. He had never given that any thought, but after quiet chats, almost as if his mother-in-law was a counsellor, he could see that lack of empathy was certainly one of symptoms of the spectrum. She was good for him because she played to his ego, telling him that that was probably the reason he was so good at IT stuff, because he had cold unemotional logic. She felt, now nearly ninety herself, that cold logic was a prerequisite for anyone in that industry.

She had turned to her daughter and suggested that perhaps she did some voluntary work to start off with, whereby she could leave when she found things too much. In that way she would still be 'getting out there' after what she had called years of repression. Olly recoiled at that. Not for one moment had he believed he had 'oppressed' his wife. He thought he had provided the ideal family life, but obviously not.

They got through it, mainly because Olly's wife loved him like nothing on earth and because she knew that every single one of his actions were, in his mind-set, designed to make life pleasant and easy for her. Most of all, she knew that he loved her in that peculiar way that Olly brought to any relationship. There was no malice; he had provided for her and the family; he had been a good father and so all that was needed was some understanding by both of them. He had agreed to listen more to her thoughts, and even if he didn't understand them, which of course he often didn't, he would still realise that they were important and the pair of them should work to resolve the issues. Olly was a man of his word. He was an honourable man, a man of principled morals. He seldom enjoyed jokes at work when they were at someone else's expense, or jokes that made fun of disabilities or gender. He was, he realised later, politically a Liberal, but principled by many old-fashioned values.

So retire from the IT department he did. He was well thought of by colleagues and friends he had made in the work place, proven by the turnout at his farewell do. He made a speech that was meant to be serious and prophetic, but people took it the wrong way and started laughing. "There was a time," he started, "when our Chief Accountant had a ledger, when his out page was nearest the window, and his income page nearest the door. But now, he is capable of knowing balances by the push of a button, he no longer has to make a pen and ink entry into an old leather bound ledger."

"Yes he does, he checks the computer output every Thursday," piped up some little brat of a trainee accountant. That started the laughter. Olly knew it was true that whilst he had tried to persuade the old bugger to ditch his ledger, the stubborn ex-RAF accountant still preferred to rely on his pen, and not the 'witchcraft' that had infused into nearly every aspect of his life. Olly consoled himself that the Chief Accountant would very soon follow him out into the pastures for sunny days of grazing in peace. But the thing that pleased him was that he actually felt love from the many people in the room, lots and lots of it. He was going to be missed.

Like so many retiring people Olly found it difficult. The sudden withdrawal of a place to go every day was a challenge. He never realised how much he missed the company, the comfort of just the occasional remark. There was also a loss of status. He was now not the IT manager, he was an OAP, the group of people lumped together by media and government alike. If you are an OAP, then that is what you are; you cannot move up the scale and become a Chief OAP, or a Senior OAP – you are stuck now, for the rest of life as being just an OAP.

He felt he had so much more to give and got involved with this local group promoting the rights of older people, with whom he now found himself drinking group coffee. They talked and talked. They talked of unfair things and fair things that had not worked out, and a tidal wave of concerns, drowning them all in what was almost depression. He became aware that, despite his knowledge of computing in its various guises, he too was falling behind. No longer at the 'coalface', his prophecy of being de-skilled after a fortnight was true. How on earth were these even older people meant to keep up? Most of them had no background in IT. Now, away from it on a daily basis, he understood much better the bewildering array of 'foreign' language pumped out by his previous industry. Why could unplugging and restarting a bloody computer repair some fault? And he now took the point that if any other industry produced such rubbish they would be laughed out of court. Imagine those who build aircraft suggesting you turn the engine off and then see if it would go again. No doubt things would get better and Olly was gradually forming the opinion that perhaps IT had been released to the great unwashed public a little too early.

Over time he formed the view that it was incumbent on the Government of the day to make sure that people were not left behind, that training and information should be readily available in centres to help people cope, and on top of that, free. This was going to be his cause, his reason for being, he told himself.

He and the others felt they had to make a stand against some of the ways of life currently washing over them and this was to be their first big publicity stunt.

"Well, frankly I'm cross with myself, I can't any longer go through life doing nothing. I have to do something like other protesters, I have to get our voices heard." He was speaking out loud now, and that scared him because he couldn't remember when he had started to speak out loud.

"My wife asked me last night what sort of statement I was about to make – what was my demand? That wasn't easy. There were so many demands, what was my priority? Frankly I don't know, and I will take advice from the others over that."

Olly's wife had not been impressed. "You come up with all these things in the world that you think are wrong, and you soppy lot are going to protest about fare levels on the Gosport Ferry."

Olly was aware that she had a point and well made: of all the issues in the world, the fare on the Gosport ferry seemed rather downmarket, but this was the vehicle he had wedded himself too, and perhaps the opportunity to make other points might come from it. Who knows, this might turn into a countrywide movement. This point he took back to his wife.

"But people in the media will see beyond that. It's a bit like the riots isn't it? The kids go on a rampage and steal large televisions out of the shops that they have just kicked the window in, but the media plant all sorts of things on it, don't they? The media go on to say the kids are deprived, that they lack education and all sorts of things like that. My guess is that the media will see our protest and we will be regarded in the same vein. They, and I mean by 'they' the media and certain politicians, will take up loads of issues that affect older people. We don't use our power enough."

"Well Olly, my love, I hope you are right. You are going to have to get to the press though, before that … that woman, what's her name, Joyce." The concerned wife continued with her worries.

"You'll all probably be taken in under some mental health provisions – no one will take you seriously. Olly, the sad fact is that no one will take you seriously in this country today unless you use some method of getting onto the media circus, and that probably involves violence of some description. So, come on, Olly, are you ready for violence, and all that would entail?"

Olly was appalled by that remark. His wife knew full well that he was opposed to all violence no matter what the cause.

"No, and you know I'm not, and to say something like that was a little unkind and below the belt, because it's not exactly like we are going to be violent, is it? I accept that we may disrupt the lives of some people, but other protesters always justify that as a means to an end, and it's all well worth it in the end. But I want to be fair, because the chances that anyone on board the ferry can change one jot of what is going on in the world is remote. So I will need to say sorry to them, to apologise, when the whole thing is over." Olly's wife looked at him, bemused. She didn't query it because she knew that was the sort of daft concept her husband would have in his head. Everyone could shake hands then and go home, and speak of what a great day everyone had had.

"Just suppose that the crew on there are trained, that they have weapons and blow you over the side - how you going to cope with that?" She was right, of course, but she could always find an excuse for doing nothing. He resolved that at some point he would actually tell her that, but not today. "And the other thing is I worry about you personally - this is making you nervous and tense, and it is doing you no good. You might just as well be back at work." The argument or debate swung from one point to another.

"Yes, yes, I know it's making me tense. I shed skin from my head when I am tense, and half my face was on the pillow this morning when I woke up. I wish you were coming with me. That would make a lot of difference to me and I would feel a lot more comfortable having you there." There was quite a long silence. He seldom referred to 'comfort' matters within their marriage, in fact he found talking about any emotion even to his wife of some forty years rather difficult.

"Look, we've been through this before. Oh Olly love, I am not coming, purely because I don't feel well enough. I think I may let you all down. But that doesn't stop me being worried for your sake, and yes I know only too well that you are worked up about it, and I suspect that one of the reasons for that is you know deep down as well as I do that you are with a load of prats, and you haven't developed any criteria on what a successful outcome looks like. It seems like you are just doing this for the sake of doing it."

She, of course, was right again and for that reason he did not challenge her. He had become aware, however, for the first time, that his wife was really quite worried about the venture and he probably owed it to her to handle the day carefully, and avoid anything that would, shall we say, prevent him coming home that night. His own thoughts went to how wilfully neglectful he had been in not establishing better communication within the group, how none of them actually understood what a successful outcome looked like, or even understood the concept. He was also causing anxiety to his wife: 'anxious wife, anxious life', he thought. He remembered his 'contract' with her, to take account of how she felt, and to a degree, Olly wrestled with the unfortunate fact that he was breaking that contract. He had convinced himself that whilst she was not coming with him in person, she would be there with him in spirit because that is what that wonderful lady did. Was this the time to put his arm around her and tell her not to worry? Olly did nothing instinctively, he always did 'nothing' instinctively. He thought about things for what seemed ages, but was probably only seconds and then launched his amazingly long arms around his wife's shoulders. He pulled her towards him, feeling for a couple seconds rather manly. "Don't worry love, I promise you that I will not do anything that gets me into trouble."

To say she was surprised would have been an understatement. Here was raw savage emotion, or as close to that as Olly was ever going to get. It was overwhelming but it was touching and she appreciated it.

"Olly, you have a wonderful way with you, thanks for that reassurance." Was she being sarcastic? Olly couldn't tell.

But now, he was seated is this rather dark cafe. It was like walking blindly into a cavern, not knowing where it came out or what faced you on the journey. The cafe's windows faced the wrong way: north. It looked up the harbour to where the Royal Navy parked the odd vessel the government still allowed it to play with. The windows looked up the harbour towards Portsdown Hill, reminding people of all the history that pervaded the whole area. These cafe windows never saw the sun, not even on a bright day like this.

The sudden influx of elderly customers had certainly taken the proprietor by surprise. Seldom had he seen a group and seldom had he had to make so many cups of coffee at the same time.

Olly liked the place, however. He could forgive the general darkness, which co-incidentally fitted his mood, because despite the chairs, despite the cheap signs run off on the proprietor's printer last night, in a font size rarely used, the coffee required no skill to order. In this establishment a black coffee was just that. A spoonful of Nescafe and some hot water. If you wanted a white one, you added milk. Same with his water: no expensive bottles that claimed minerals and other rare ingredients that increased your sperm output or some other wild attribute, The water came out the tap, ever so simple and was even called Portsmouth Water.

He was growing to like the proprietor, who was miserable; the man was not even cheered up by the loaded wallets that had just entered his establishment. His apron was clean enough, but every time he lifted his arm he exposed a huge damp patch under the armpit. Olly was put off a bit by that, but enormously cheered when Joyce demanded a herbal tea. This was going to be fun, he thought!

"Don't do herbals."

"What, not at all?"

"That's right madam, not at all. No demand for them here, in fact there's not a lot of demand for anything most days."

Olly was surprised by the remark; he would have thought a cafe in such a location would be constantly used and a business no-brainer.

"Oh for Pete's sake." She realised there was no husband currently to fall back on, because despite her apparent dominance, she did look to him for back-up in situations like this.

"Tell you what, I have some mint out the back. I was going to knock up some mint sauce for the lamb at lunchtime. I could cut some of that up and put it in boiling water."

"Thank you, I will try that," Joyce said, trying to keep her dignity.

She always got taller when she was affronted; her shoulders went back and her neck stiffened.

The proprietor had actually tried. He had cut up the mint, the fresh mint one may add, and soaked it, so to some degree she should be grateful.

"Do you want me to strain off the mint leaves, love?"

"No, don't bother, I dare say it will continue infusing."

"What?"

"Infusing …getting stronger then," she said, realising that he did not understand 'infusing'.

"Oh, OK." he said, looking at her as though she had come from outer space.

"So how much is that then?"

"Oh, I dunno, give us fifty pence."

Joyce was delighted. She felt instantly better seeing as the others had all paid a pound plus for their coffees. She was more than delighted with the price and assured the proprietor that she would sing his praises around the town of Gosport. Olly was not sure whether the proprietor thought this was a good thing or a bad thing, but the man had just smiled.

Olly sat with Joyce; after all, he thought, someone had to. The only problem was that Olly could not quite take her seriously; every time she opened her mouth bits of mint had stuck fast to her teeth. Some people would pay a lot of money for that, he thought - she could have inadvertently created a brand new fashion. Quite pretty really.

CHAPTER 3

Hardy was considerably flustered when eventually he almost stumbled into the cafe. He was moist all over his body with sweat, his face was bright red and he was somewhat breathless. He had hurried, even though 'his people' had told him there was no need for that, when pointing out to him that they had all day. Hardy, however, felt the need to hurry because he was the source of the delay. For him, it highlighted the issue with the group, that they did indeed think they had all day. He needed to set an example and show them that time was important and a sense of some timekeeping was required.

Hardy felt the delay 'he was causing' would also make the others more nervous. It would have given them time to think about things and maybe change their minds about the day, thus backing out. This was always the problem with volunteers, he reasoned – they couldn't be relied upon!

"Crikey Hardy, you look like you are about to collapse."

"Bloody 'ell, I think he needs an ambulance more than the ferry," added Kenneth.

"I'm fine, I'll be alright. Come on let's get on with this."

Bert had the banner, which he collected under his arm again. It was a substantial banner; he had painted on the back of one that had previously been used by some young Liberal Democrats. It had been kind of the Lib Dems to let him use it. Joyce picked up her bag. She gave the impression of not being on speaking terms with Hardy again, cocking her head at an angle whilst moving away from Hardy, giving a body language signal. No one took much notice of that; they all knew by now that could change as quickly as a cloud obscuring the sun on a windy day.

They just missed a ferry, in fact their timing could not have been worse. There was no sight in the world that Portsmouth and Gosport people dreaded more than seeing the backside of the ferry just leaving the pontoon – it meant, when they were only running one ferry, that you could do nothing for the next fifteen minutes but sit and wait. You could see it, but you couldn't touch it, it was going away from you and suddenly you had lost control of your world. You couldn't chase it, you couldn't shout at the driver, and you couldn't call it back. It could feel like rejection, it could sometimes even feel deliberate, but of course it was not. And for the group now gathered on the pontoon it meant their nervous energy was now kicking in big-time. Olly was pacing up and down; he was tall and still stood very upright. Kenneth, Ken and Bert leant on the stainless steel railing, watching as the craft ploughed its way over to Portsmouth.

Joyce and Hardy stood together, but they were not together. As was usually the case she was fed up with the man in her life constantly – in her opinion – showing her up. There was plenty of room on the pontoon; she could have stood anywhere but she still elected to stand within striking distance of her husband.

"I'll never understand those two," Ken commented to Kenneth.

"No, I don't think they understand each other, so I wouldn't try, Ken."

Joyce

Joyce and Hardy were childless, but not out of choice. Years and years ago, examinations showed that she could not have children. This in itself was bad news, but the additional sting for Joyce was that the 'failure' was down to her. She had convinced herself and close friends that it was Hardy that had been 'firing blanks'. The realisation that it was indeed her health was painful socially as well as personally. Consequently she had neither corrected nor denied the situation to other people. These days, they would have probably been able to do something about it, but back then, it was not possible. This particular issue and its associated regret at not having children would haunt both Joyce and Hardy for the majority of their marriage.

Soon after the news that Joyce could not conceive, they had talked about adoption but Hardy was set against it, saying things like 'it would not be his blood'. She actually did understand his argument and had some sympathy with it, but she had chosen to take a different stance. The refusal to adopt had given her years of ammunition to use against him. She had yet again transferred the responsibility for 'no children' to Hardy. It was his fault because he had rejected the adoption route to parenthood. The situation had eaten into their relationship. Mentally they had drifted apart to the point she felt she was no longer really with him. Their relationship appeared to any outsider, once they got to know them, and to Joyce herself, as just a habit. They were staying together because she had nowhere else to go.

Joyce was not stupid, however, and deep down she understood that she was just as much to 'blame' as he was for the unfortunate state of their relationship. Why had she said the things she had? This question revolved in her head like clothes in a spin dryer. At first she had not meant to hurt him; indeed the more she thought about things, she did not actually mean to hurt anyone at any time. But she always seemed to achieve just that: hurt. There was always that burning resentment that smouldered away inside her that sometimes came out like a volcano erupting. Releasing the anger often resulted in indifference to other people's feelings which sometimes came across as damned right offensive.

Joyce assumed she had probably 'lived' more than anyone in the group, and she was not always proud of it. She did not endear herself to other females who at best described her as rude, and now in older age she could not flirt with men like she used to. It had in all honesty mainly been no more than flirtation. In reality, she thought, she was probably just as lonely as Bert. She remembered some years ago telling another female acquaintance that you can be lonely in a marriage, and she felt she was.

She had been a stunner when she met Hardy. She had gone to work for him as a PA / secretary. Hardy had his own business repairing and supplying parts to the motor sports trade, and as such he got to go to lots of trade events that also provided additional social 'do's' afterwards. It had not taken him long to offer to take her along as his guest, and she loved it. Often she would be centre of attention from the many men that attended. These were macho males, who previously that day had donned white overalls or wore helmets and leathers. Lots of wives would shun her, seeing her as a threat, but the clever ones made friends with her, using the motto 'keep your challengers close so you know what's happening'. Early in the relationship, however, whilst she flirted, she was always with Hardy and she never actually strayed. She had her eye set on the main chance of securing her future with Hardy, the top man, the owner of a business. But now, many years later, she queried in her head whether she had ever actually loved him or whether she just loved the situation he was offering.

During the early days of the marriage she did everything properly; she hosted social occasions and kept his business in good shape. She kept house and cooked - they had done the right thing and invited all relatives to the wedding with no problems, and everything looked rosy in the garden.

Then, to the subject of children, that driver, that treacherous function of nature that provides the only reason for being, according to the Bible. It is the driver that takes over every living thing on the planet, and in humans becomes obsessive and ubiquitous. They planned to have two, well she did. Hardy went along with that for a quiet life, and it was, after all, what one did. It was after twelve months that she queried the non-arrival of a swelling womb. They needed to do it more often, she decided, and she worked out her ovulation programme. Hardy was required to 'make love' for an eight-day period around those dates.

It got to the point where Hardy dreaded her going off up stairs with her thermometer. At the right temperature it was time to begin the 'mating' process and she would shout down the stairs, "Hardy, Hardy, it's time." By day eight, he'd had it, and after several months of this, the inevitable had happened: Hardy was just unable to 'service' her. She remembered this failure, and it had angered her tremendously. Her reaction was quite contrary to advice provided by the 'help' columns in various women's magazines. She began to make a joke of him. The effect had been that he lost interest in sex completely. She got more and more angry as she noticed that her aim of children was fading. In her mind, her man had been no good for the job.

She had not been consciously aware that her flirting with other men had got worse, and even in front of Hardy she would openly display 'come on's' to other men. It seemed never to bother Hardy, in fact in a peculiar way he was rather turned on by it, particularly when the guys came back at her. It was amusing to see her back down. But one night she didn't back down. They had been to a dinner dance organised by one of the firms he did business with. The usual somewhat over-intoxicated men got her up for dances, fast ones, and made advances to her even though Hardy was sitting at the table looking miserable. One came and sat with them; he was less drunk than the others, but by now Joyce had had a few and was becoming a little stupid. Like always, the music slowed down towards the end of the evening and the guy she was with at least had the good grace to ask Hardy if she was 'available' to dance with. "Help yourself mate, not up to me," he had said in a semi-resentful manner.

The pair had started off their dancing relatively far apart, but within minutes she had her arms round his neck and they were very close. Hardy was more concerned about his own ego than anything else. The people round the floor could see this guy was coming onto her big time, and when she did not remove his hand from her backside, Hardy could not wait for the dance to end, and thus end his embarrassment, but 'Lady in Red' played for what seemed forever.

He never did see the going of them; they sort of disappeared from the dance floor and she did not join Hardy in their hotel room until way past 4am. It annoyed her that he asked no questions, showed no emotion, no reaction whatsoever. God, was she cross.

He was, however, angry that it had come to this, that her obsession with becoming pregnant had got to the point where she could easily destroy the nest she had built to bring a baby into. It was illogical to him, and when she thought about it, it was illogical to her as well. He never asked her about what happened that night because he didn't want confirmation of what he already suspected, and when nothing came of it, he saw little point in pursuing the issue. In retrospect he should have; he should have been angry, sad and frustrated, and he was all of those things but never said a word, simply because in a strange sort of way it gave him the upper hand. When several months later she had received the results of the medical tests, he was almost on a high. That was a goal that was not easy to achieve with Joyce, and he revelled in it for a short while. Joyce never really came to terms with it.

Now years later, Joyce had a Road-to-Damascus moment. For goodness sake, they were both as miserable as sin. Hardy could not stand her nowadays - he made that more and more clear - and to be frank, for the vast majority of the time she could not stand him. They were a habit more than a marriage, she would tell herself; he had lost all his excitement, and probably so had she. Any touching in the matrimonial bed was totally accidental. She mostly undressed in the bathroom and was keen to cover up on return to the bedroom, not that he was watching anyway. Hardy had lost desire, well for her at least. Did he see other women whom he fancied? He did fancy other women but he had never done anything about it. He did, however, keep it a mystery from Joyce and he rather enjoyed it. In turn Joyce had the opinion that if he did approach another woman, she would soon find there was not a lot in it for her.

So the big question that hit her was why they were both still together? There were no children to worry about, indeed nothing to worry about.

At breakfast four months before today's event, she had come out with it.

"I've been thinking," she announced with a suitable amount of drama.

Joyce thinking was always an alarming thought for Hardy, so he did actually look up from the extremely healthy muesli that she fed him, indicating to him that she did actually care about his health.

"I've decided that I have had enough of this rotten marriage. This is misery for both of us, and has been for years. I'm putting an end to it. I am going to see about a divorce."

Hardy could only respond with: "What do you mean, you are going to see about a divorce?" He knew exactly what she meant but this was the only thing he could say that gave him some thinking time. He had not expected anything like this, and it was shaking him.

"I am going to see a solicitor and find out about us splitting up properly, so I am free of you once and for all."

"Oh right." Well what else could he say, he reasoned. Her arguments were right; they almost hated each other and it had got worse since he had given up the business. He was under her feet all day, and no visible reason for even being there. When they ran the business, there was a reason to be there; he was doing something and in that environment he was the boss, at least in name. He had status. People would ask for him and she would accept that.

But now, the business had gone, now she pretty much ruled the roost in their home.

"So, what am I meant to do now then? Do I have to find a solicitor as well?"

That was pathetic, and he knew it.

"That's up to you isn't it?"

"Well not really, I am probably going to be forced into it by your actions."

"Most probably, but whatever you do, I have made up my mind, we cannot go on like this - it is hell on earth."

Hardy could not argue that one. It was hell but had never thought of actually ending it. It was a situation that he needed to think through a bit, and one that she had probably already done. Questions started to flood his head, not least the prospect of being on his own for the first time in forty-odd years.

"So, when you seeing this solicitor?" he asked.

"I don't know yet, I haven't yet made an appointment. I thought I would be fair to you and tell you first - after all, I do realise that it is a big step."

"A fucking big step I would call it." The first signs of anger appeared in Hardy. He decided to leave the remains of his muesli and get out of the room.

He went to where he always went when they were having a row, to the garage. He had a seat there, a very worn brown seat that whilst offering comfort, also smelt of years of use, a mixture of oil and human sweat: a well-cultivated smooth blackened surface had been left by constant use across many parts of the chair. It had been employed in his business for years, in fact so far back he could not remember where it came from. The chair did what it had always done, it cradled him, almost saying "there, there, everything will be alright". Hardy, however, somehow knew that this was different. Joyce was not angry, she was not upset, she was not being vindictive: she was, after so many years, being pragmatic and that's what made this situation different from all the other times he had sat in this chair reflecting on her words.

The solicitor was a little man, a balding little man. His shirtsleeves were far too long and seemed to impede his movement across his desk. The cuffs, although fastened with expensive cuff links, were grubby, as was his dark tie that showed the odd spot of what appeared to be tomato ketchup. He would not have done well at Crufts International dog show either, sporting an overshot jaw, which caused him to spray many of his words. He obviously still used cream of some kind on his little bit of black but greying hair, but he smiled and he was gentle and nice.

Her initial statement, as she was saying it, felt weird to her: "I want to divorce my husband." The words 'my husband' seemed to echo in her ears and became distant, as if it wasn't her really saying this at all. Mr Balding Man was obviously used to this. His reaction was unemotional, unsurprised and businesslike, which should not have surprised her. Joyce had expected a "oh dear" at least, just to add to her sense of drama, but no such exclamation was forthcoming: this, of course, was an everyday experience for him. Instead of drama she got:

"OK, well, look, I see lots of men and women come in here requesting help to divorce their spouse, and I always say to them, contrary to what you might expect, that I don't really want to help. I can do without the normal rush for your custom. On all levels, and not being rude, particularly with you older people, divorce is a tragedy, an absolute disaster. Regardless of how much you have thought this through, I assure you it is going to be a major trauma for you as well as your husband." He stopped; it seemed to Joyce that it was the letter T that encouraged saliva to spray somewhat. He wiped his chin with the back of his hand.

"What grounds have you for this relationship breakdown?" he eventually continued.

Joyce had not been expecting such a lecture, albeit short, and was a little taken aback. And she had also not thought about this latest question of his. This took several seconds to process.

Grounds! Grounds! Of course, why hadn't she thought of that? Even today, you can't just turn up at some office and say you want to divorce - you have to have some sort of reason even if it was made up.

"Well, er um, yes, relationship breakdown I suppose. I mean we just argue and argue, and these days he can't even do that very well."

"OK, Joyce." A bit too familiar she thought. She didn't like this first-name fad that seem to pervade all officialdom nowadays. "I am going to go through this with you very carefully, then I want you to go away and think about it for forty-eight hours or so, and come back and see me when you have thought it through fully understanding what this means both to you." Her solicitor had taken on a fatherly role, and to be fair, she thought, one that suited him. He was, obviously well practised in this lecture.

"You need to have clear thoughts on the current matrimonial home. Most courts if it comes to dispute will order the home to be sold, especially when no children are involved. I take it that no children are involved and no one else lives with you?" Joyce nodded.

"We never had children," she quickly added.

"OK, well that makes things a bit easier. So you would need to arrange with your husband for three options. He buys you out, you buy him out or lastly the place is sold and the proceeds split equally. So do you have a rough idea of how much your place is worth?"

"Oh God, I haven't given that much of a thought. I suppose three hundred thousand or something like that."

"Well, that's not bad, so if you get two hundred and ninety-five thousand for it, and we will make an assumption that there is no capital gains tax to pay on it, after costs you will probably end up with two hundred and ninety thousand, which is about one hundred and forty-five thousand each. For that you could achieve a rather nice one-bed flat or something like that. Then we have other assets like furniture and perhaps even the car that has to be taken account of.

We then come to ongoing financial matters. Does your husband have a pension?"

"Oh yes, he paid in for years from the business."

"Well we could go for half of that, but of course he could go for half of yours, but one word of warning that if he should pre-decease you, all entitlement would be lost to any of his income.

"Another issue is the state pension, which is often not looked at in divorce. Individuals must have 35 years of National Insurance credits to be entitled to the full state pension of around £8,000 a year. For every year they are below this they lose one 35th of their entitlement.

"If the wife is a non-earner, and stopped work at a reasonably early age, the chances are she will not have 35 years of NI credits," said the balding solicitor

"I say to all women to get a pension forecast before divorce, and if they have not got the full state pension and they have got to pay for some years of backlog, that will be paid for out of the divorce pot rather than her money, as the chances are it was a joint decision for her to be a stay-at-home wife."

"Ah," Joyce replied, mainly because she was getting too much information to absorb in one session. Joyce was beginning to wonder whether the balding solicitor actually knew how old she was. She was already receiving her state pension, but she decided not to tell him that at this point. She was quite flattered.

"We took the decision to, shall we say, right back then to fiddle not paying national insurance for me - we couldn't afford it at the time, so my credits were almost nothing."

"Right, so therein lies another issue that we would need to clarify."

Joyce noted the cash register in his eyes at this point. She also anticipated many denials from Hardy. He would want the car, he would want this and that, and she could see a fight on the horizon. This was not going to be easy.

"I want also to touch on other issues that you may not have thought about. As I said first off, don't underestimate the trauma this is going to cause you. Think it through - you are going to find life hard financially, and don't underestimate just how much you still interact with your husband on a daily basis."

"Huh," she said to that.

"It will, of course, be even more difficult for him. He probably does not have the support networks that you do, and of course his confidence will be severely knocked. I suspect that you would still attract a male friend, but for him it will not be so easy."

"I have no wish to attract another male, I can assure you of that." She was almost offended at the thought.

"Well, you may say that now, but things change when you are on your own constantly. You don't realise just how much saying good night means, or at night no one to cuddle."

"And no one to wake you up every two hours when they get up for a pee, no one to clean up after when you get up in the morning and find the bastard has missed the toilet pan at least twice in the night. No one belching and farting, no one to tell you they have heart burn again because they've cleared half a bottle of scotch. Oh yes, I'll miss it alright."

The little balding fat solicitor realised that this was one angry lady, but he seen it all before and held his line.

"Most of all, think what accommodation you can afford, and as I said before, it is better if you both move out and sell; that is the cleanest of breaks. Most certainly that is what his legal people will be advising him."

Those words suddenly jarred: "The cleanest of breaks." Well she would still see him, she added; there was no point in them not being, well, friends she supposed.

"I doubt it. In my experience there is so much bitterness and resentment. It is very difficult to avoid that. And of course for younger people, it is often the children that puts a certain amount of pressure on them to stay good friends."

Joyce left the fat balding, slightly moist solicitor with the long sleeves, in a different mood to the one she had arrived with. She was more pensive, and some of the things he had said did in fact require more thought. When she got home, Hardy was out. 'Out', she thought, the man is never 'out', he has nowhere to go, well not without her. He must be doing something like going to get some petrol, but why would he suddenly do that without her?

Hang on, she thought, why am I bothered? He'll be on his own for good later, once I've divorced him.

The day wore on, and it got to just after five, and Hardy had not returned home. She was confident that he would return by five-fifteen because he never missed Pointless on the telly. She was reluctant to ring him on his mobile; that would show a sign of weakness she thought, and he might get the wrong impression.

At five-thirty she rang his mobile. She heard it ring; it was in the kitchen. That made her cross again - how many times had she told him to take his mobile with him, and how many times had he failed to do so? He didn't seem to place the same importance on it as she did.

The time waiting for the ferry to return from Portsmouth passed so slowly: it always did when you were waiting. Bert noted that the 'young' had their mobile phones, and most of the people on the pontoon had become engrossed in what their little screens displayed.

For Bert it was one of the burdens of modern day life, waiting. You waited at traffic lights, in banks, in supermarkets, in doctor's surgeries, in hospitals and dentist's. You waited in for the gas man, you waited for a win on the premium bonds, wishing another month away until the next draw, and for Vodafone to answer the phone, and most of all, you waited at airports. He hated airports - impersonal, uncaring and frustrating. Why, he would ask, if he misses the plane he is late, but if the airline fails its time for take-off or arrival, it is 'delayed'? And then there seemed no end to the souls that could be crammed into that steel tube, bringing on bags of enormous proportions, and mainly succeeding to squeeze them into overhead lockers, blocking the onward transmission of those behind them, who had to wait! Bert had once calculated that he had spent nearly 900 days of his life just waiting, and if you added that to sleeping, assuming eight hours per night for let's say eighty years, you slept for nine thousand seven hundred and thirty-three days. So that was just over twenty-nine years of your life, totally wasted.

But as sure as the tide itself, the ferry returned, spewing forth its passengers, and reloading.

They filed on, their tickets being clipped, no suspicion whatsoever so far. The operation would need to be carried out on the upper deck, near the bridge. It was, then, a bonus that the day was warm and sunny; no one would welcome doing this in the wind and rain. Bert needed help. His legs were not able to cope with the stairs. Ken stood behind him, which he somewhat regretted as the best way to assist him was to literally push his backside upwards, thus taking the weight off the thighs, so that Kenneth could manoeuvre one step at a time Bert's leg in an upward motion.

The 'mate', a crew member who had just untied the vessel, needed to get up the very same steps to the bridge, as he had now closed the gate, let go, and they were on their way over. They knew the mate always returned to the bridge, and that was an essential part of the plan. But the mate was stuck behind a struggling Bert on this narrow stairway to the upper deck, with the two Kens, who were trying to help him.

"Are you people all right? What are you trying to do?" asked the mate. The effect was immediate. The question 'what are you trying to do.' seemed much more important and alarming than it probably should have. They had been rumbled: the show was up, it was over before it had even begun. Only one of the three could turn to respond. Bert was incapable of turning round, and Kenneth in the lead could not see the mate round the now stuck and terrified

Bert. In fact Bert now panicked, and when he panicked he passed wind, uncontrollably. Ken, at this point, was standing behind him with his hand on Bert's backside in an effort to offset some of Bert's weight. The mate just said:

"Gawd, look, do you need help? You don't have to go up top, you could just stay down here in the lounge or outside on the quarterdeck. Why do you so want to get to the upper deck, when it is so difficult for you?"

"It's such a nice day, and I so want to see the views of the harbour just once more."

"Eh?" asked the mate.

Somehow, they had to think of a good reason to go to the upper deck. In their three minds this was becoming a crisis. Bert decided on telling a version of the truth. But it both hurt and worried him as he said the words. Replying to the mate he could be foretelling his actual future.

"See, I've been diagnosed with cancer. I don't know how long I have left or how long I will be mobile and these kind gentlemen have volunteered to help me see Portsmouth Harbour from the ferry. I have taken so much for granted - the ferry has been there all my life and for just, well perhaps, one last time, I wanted to be on the upper deck."

The mate, even though he gave an outward impression of being very tough, with large powerful shoulders, black hair and a healthy tan with the compulsory sunglasses, was moved to help. Who would not have been? He would take charge of this and ensure the man had his last wish honoured.

"Look sir, come away, let me get behind him." The mate exerted considerably more power than Ken, who by now was not only impressed with Bert's quick thinking but also overcome by Bert's sulphur-like exhaust gases. But Bert did have cancer. He had not lied, and that was important......

somehow, he must be forgiven for the lack of control of his sphincter muscles.

The mate delivered Bert to the upper deck. The others stood there astounded at the unexpected difficulty that had arisen surrounding Bert's mobility.

It was now more important that they got their timings right, so they needed to note where each other was, and the position of the ferry. And that was part of the problem now, because the Portsmouth pontoon was already now only yards away

"Right, this is it, men," announced Olly. "Everyone ready?"

"Of course, come on, let's just do it." An almost unanimous response.

"Right, I will go and talk to the Captain." At long last it seemed that Hardy could find no reason for not actually doing this, apart from the fact his heart was pounding like an earthquake and he found he could now hardly speak. Joyce was aware of his nerves; she had seen this many times over the years. She was right. Hardy stood rooted to the spot, not moving.

"Typical, absolutely typical, I knew this would happen, he's going to back out."

"No no, he's not, just leave him. Don't wind him up now at this point, Joyce, we need to back him not keep criticising," said an alarmed Ken

"You don't have to live with it do you, Ken? I get this all the time, right through our marriage I've had this, promises and promises, that never come to anything."

"Oh, shut up, just bloody shut up!" Hardy was now annoyed again and had resorted to the usual plea to end her tirade. It had never worked in the past and it didn't work now.

"Don't you tell me to shut up - it's about time people knew the truth about you. You're all talk, you always have been. Honesty Olly, you don't know half of it."

Olly became somewhat concerned that he was about to be told half of it, and that would use up time, valuable time that they just did not have. The crossing was four-and-a-half minutes at the most and they needed to do something pretty damned quick.

Olly took a decision.

"OK, if you are not doing it, I am."

At this, Hardy became annoyed not only with Joyce, but also at himself and Olly. In fact he was cross with everyone, but counted to ten.

"No, I will do it as arranged."

With that, he turned, and headed towards the few steps that led up to the bridge. He shouted to the others: "OK everyone, it's on - take up your positions."

Olly went to the steps with Hardy, while the others crowded round the steps to prevent others getting up or down.

"You're not allowed up here, sir. See that sign? No public access." The mate was polite but firm.

"Look, I need to speak to the Captain, urgently."

"We're just coming into the Portsea pontoon sir; it will have to wait a couple of minutes, then he will be available, in the meantime, I've got to go down and tie up. Excuse me." And with that he pushed his way past them, and that was that.

This wasn't going to plan. The combination of the debate with Joyce and Bert's struggle up the stairs had lost them valuable time and there was now no way they could take any form of action coming alongside again. Hardy felt he had no choice but to let the chap down the steps to go about his duty.

"Stand down everyone," he shouted. The mate gave him a peculiar look that Hardy found hard to interpret, but it had a look, he thought, of 'nutter'. Hardy had little time to consult. They would all have to get off as you were only allowed to stay on the ferry for one journey when you were expected to disembark. Had the crew spotted what they were up to? Were they now marked men...and women of course. Had the police already been alerted? This was all going wrong and so quickly. Bert was struggling to undo the banner and now he had to do it up again, all very stressful for the man.

"Hardy ... Hardy." Olly was calling him. Bert was having the same trouble getting down the steps, but the caring mate came to his rescue this time early enough to get him down and off the vessel.

"Don't panic, let's all get off and regroup. The day is still young and we have plenty of time left," comforted Hardy, not really sure whether he meant it or not.

"So let's be honest, this attempt has failed," said Sarah, in what appeared a matter-of-fact way.

"Let's all go and have a nice cup of tea, and try again in a half an hour or something." Her influence was calming and made sense. Bert agreed, with a "'hear hear." So they all got off, and shuffled up the pontoon.

"So, where we going?" Ken enquired. He was head of the pack at this point and had realised they were all just following him. He did not wish to be responsible for the final destination at this point.

"I don't know, let's just find somewhere to get a cup of tea or something." Bert almost pleaded. He was still carrying his rolled-up banner, having had no chance to unfurl it. It was fairly heavy, being made of a canvas and somehow waterproofed. It was causing irritation to his shoulder, making it more difficult to walk with his walking stick. He was, to a degree, still suffering from the humiliation of the stair incident. This whole thing was beginning to take it out of him.

The railway station buffet appeared the easiest place, and that way they would be able to observe any unusual activity regarding police, and so the magnificent seven trooped into the buffet. As usual on a station in England, the place was generally unwelcoming, dull and with a limited array of produce. At least it had the advantage of being close to the worn-out toilets however, if indeed they were open.

"It's better we sit on the platform rather than in here," Joyce said, and with that carried out her well-drilled routine of bagging seven chairs around one quite inadequate table. She placed various articles on the chairs to indicate to any other member of the public that those seats were taken. Indeed, her look of possession would have frightened any man away and it would have taken a woman of equal substance to offer resistance.

Bert was first to return, with no drink because Kenneth was getting it for him. He did not relish sitting next to Joyce but had no real choice when she beckoned him.

"You know," he started, "this is one of the most exciting things I have ever done in my life, and more than that, I feel it's possibly the first time I have ever made a stand over anything. I have often threatened to, but never have, do you know?"

"What's so different now?" Joyce asked cautiously. She could see things were going to take some time before the others returned, and she might even get an answer she didn't want.

"Well, I think it's like everything, when things affect you,

you suddenly feel you've got to fight for what is right or, of course, what I think is right. I need to do it now, you know - we should all do things now. Tomorrow may not be available to us. Have I told you about my illness?" She had no time to reply. "It started with a cramp-like pain in my stomach. I took the usual stuff, you know like Gaviscon, and Syrup of Figs, and I thought a good ... well you know, a good go on the toilet would be all that it needed. But it didn't go away, did it? It stayed like that.

"After several days, I was getting to the point where by I was doubled over with this damned pain. Mrs Burgess, have you met her? She lives next door, has done for years, reckoned I should ring the doctor. Well that seemed quite sensible I suppose, so I rang. They told me after about ten minutes of waiting that if I needed an urgent appointment I would have to ring between eight and nine the following morning. Well to be honest, I wasn't sure whether it was urgent or not. I mean you don't like to get in the way of those who are really sick, and I thought I just had a tummy ache. They told me there were no ordinary appointments available, so I just thanked them for the care they had shown and left it." He paused for breath.

"Mrs Burgess was very cross when I told her - she said I should be seen straight away. I always remember when mother was ill, must have been in the mid 1960s, and I went to the telephone box to ring for old Doctor Rowe, his nurse said he would pop round after surgery, and he did, and he diagnosed appendix problems, got her taken into hospital straight away you know, she was operated straight away." He stopped to draw breath again.

Joyce was sitting bolt upright, superior to all, her coloured gold hair added further to her height, and Bert wondered if she was listening, or indeed if she was listening, was there any interest? He intended to go on, because she had asked a question about three minutes ago, and he felt that she was entitled to a full answer. At this point he was merely scene setting.

"Of course the issue became more serious, when on the Saturday I could not lift myself out of bed. I tell you, Joyce, I became frightened. My phone is downstairs - I don't have one of those mobile things, they seem to me to be intrusive, but of course this was one time when I could have done with one. I got to my bedroom window, and shouted. Fortunately Mr Burgess was going to the bin and he asked what was up. They called an ambulance then and very kindly let the men in, because they've always had a key, you know. Anyway, they got me into Queen Alexandra hospital over at Cosham and it turned out, to cut a long story short, that I had a blockage caused by a growth. Now you see, I thought I paid the NHS to deal with pain and then deal with the causes of it, and then get you right. But of course it doesn't work like that, does it?"

Joyce regarded that as a rhetorical question, but debated in her head whether she should get involved in a more active way. She had, in her terms, been given far too much information for her own comfort already, without encouraging the conversation to move into more political regions. Bert was in flow and continued without her reply anyway.

"We used to get told off in local government when we got things wrong, but everyone seems frightened to say anything to these medical people. They were quite frank about it - I would have died and still could from it. They are giving me treatment now, but I think I agree with all of you, the service is just not good enough and something must be done. That reminds me, I think it's time for another pill. I'll take it with my tea when Kenneth brings it out."

She knew he was a bachelor and that he lived alone, and she realised that to be taken ill like that in such circumstances must have been quite frightening.

"Have you never been married, Bert?"

"No, no. no. The opportunity has never presented itself. In fact I think I have ever only asked one woman out in the whole of my life. I am very shy, you know, or was … I still am, and in fact I suspect I am gabbling on now because I am shy. Probably it wasn't a good idea to live with mother for so long. She did everything for me and I suppose life was too comfortable and of course I was way into my fifties when she died and too set in my ways. I had the house, no brothers or sisters to worry about and I knew everyone in the neighbourhood. I had my job in the town hall rent office and knew it backwards, and I decided, subconsciously, I suppose, not to put myself outside any comfort zone. A wife is entirely different to a mother, I understood that, and of course some men may have got it wrong and suffered later."

"I see, so you are quite selfish then really." He had not expected that response.

"Why?" It was a genuine enquiry.

"Well, in a way, you had everything, but didn't want to share with anyone at that point. So now you are a lonely old man aren't you? You reap what you sow."

Bloody hell, Bert thought, this woman is as hard as nails. Could she not offer one bit of sympathy? He said nothing for a bit; he had never viewed his life before in the focus of being selfish.

He had friends in the church and they had never mentioned him being selfish. He gave regularly to charity, so that wasn't selfish. But the truth of it was that since his illness he had indeed felt very alone. He had never felt as vulnerable as when he was staggering from his bed that morning, and it was pure luck that Mrs Burgess was within earshot.

Bert had no intention of defending any corner. He knew Joyce well enough to know that he would be in for a bruising confrontation, and on top of that he would probably come off worse in any case. So his next question was not calculated to hurt; it was nothing more than just an enquiry really.

"So, did you get married just for company and someone to take care of you?"

Joyce's retort was edged with anger and malice. She did not see it as just a polite enquiry, more a barbed comment provoked by her previous remarks and a challenge to her life habits at the moment. When she had married Hardy, things had been different: there was once love and lust, she reasoned, but not now, and she answered as things stood now.

"Well if I did, I didn't get it, did I?"

Bert chose not to answer; it would only get him into more trouble, and in any case with that remark she had got up saying she was going to help carry the drinks over. He had plenty to think about resulting from the rather short encounter. She had managed in a few seconds to throw his whole life into some sort of discussion pot. He had never looked at life through the prism of success measures, but then in a funny sort of way perhaps he should have done - after all, the church he attended every Sunday preached that you would be challenged on the day of reckoning as to what you'd done.

His brain worked overtime. He was in his head building up a sort of account - after all, he might not have that long to think about it. His cancer was by no means cured and he had little faith that it would be. He'd not been bad, but then the question now was had he been good?

He escaped doing much at all during his National Service: the army knew National Service was coming to an end when he had been called up, and had little time for the men who did not want to be there, and in turn they really didn't want to be there either. He never gave blood, he never put in collection boxes, although he did send five pounds to Children in Need one year. He kept his property up well, he was polite to his neighbours, and he was a loyal friend when he made one. He worshiped his God every Sunday, regularly and put into the collection. He was not lustful, he had never coveted his neighbour's ass, nor come to think about it his neighbour's wife's ass, or his car or his house or … no, he never had a manservant anyway. He didn't blaspheme, or masturbate excessively, and when he did do that, he always imagined a loving relationship within a marital home. He would imagine a loving wife, who would wrap her arms around him and move down his body to those parts that gave such thrills.

Recently he had not kept himself up together, and he would be the first to admit that he carried too much weight, or he had done until the last few months. He was now beginning to lose weight but for all the wrong reasons. He convinced himself that he was well respected in the community, and had been at work in the little office. His fellow workers, mainly female, had taken a mothering stance towards him, one which he did little to combat. There had been an element of formality in the office, not that it was stuffy, because they often had times of sheer laughter, of jokes and fun, and he had joined in stuff that turned somewhat raunchy. Women had changed in his lifetime; they came out with things now that only men would have said when he was younger. But he had always been respectful, perhaps even going so far as to say he was a bit frightened of women generally. That loving wife of his imagination was exactly that, a product of his imagination. Joyce had provoked thoughts which now raced through his mind. He would need to park them, however, for the moment and perhaps examine them later tonight.

Now he was involved with these people, people that he had met at church of all places, and he was about to break the law by any stretch of the imagination for the first time - at least knowingly for the first time - in his life. But perhaps today was his bit of doing good, of making a difference because Joyce, however horrible she came across, probably is right: he had been selfish, thinking only of himself and how he appeared to others.

Now, this moment might change all that.

CHAPTER 4

Kenneth

Kenneth realised that these unplanned delays in the operation were threatening his timeline to get back home by five o'clock. He would need to be back at that time because of certain care duties he needed to perform for his wife Helen. He loved his wife very much and he would not let her down for the sake of this campaign.

The group had assured him that everything would be over by four pm at the latest, but now this second hold-up, due frankly to the group's total incompetence, put the whole thing on the verge of farce and gave them little time to achieve anything much. Now, his thoughts drew him to think why on earth he was doing this. It now seemed completely crazy as well as impractical, with such a group of 'has beens'. It of course begged the question, was he included in the term 'has been?' He liked to think not, mainly because he was still earning money, albeit very little. He convinced himself he was not completely dependant on pensions. He advised people on money issues. In reality, he was a salesman attempting to sell financial products to older people.

Kenneth and Helen had returned to the United Kingdom two years previously, after living in Spain. They had spent the previous fourteen years in Spain, or as Kenneth often explained to others, in Catalunya.

"Oh the Catalans hate being called Spanish - they see themselves as a very separate people. There are many hand-painted signs in places like Girona and Figueres that say, strangely in English, that Catalunya is not Spain. Indeed, there is a huge independence movement in Catalunya, which wants total independence from the Spanish state, and to some degree, I can understand why. All the other autonomous regions of the Spanish state collect their own taxes and pay to the state on demand. In the case of Catalunya, the state takes the lot and gives them back what it thinks it deserves," explained Kenneth to any member of the group who showed an interest.

Kenneth, however, had often got involved in debate with Catalans, well, those that spoke English that is, about the issues surrounding independence. He, like many Brits living abroad, had a mere smattering of Spanish and even less of Catalan. Most of them worked on the principle that if you added volume to your English, the 'foreign' person would understand. It seldom worked.

Kenneth would query with Catalan people the pure pragmatism of 'going it alone', with their fetish for independence. How it would work in reality with things like defence, and belonging to the EU, which the Catalans thought would be their right. He enjoyed the debate, always assuming the superior nature that Brits abroad had a tendency to do. Was it because we had an aircraft carrier and a frigate, and they didn't? Or did it go deeper than that, Kenneth wondered, when the attitude had been pointed out to him.

Health, family and economic uncertainty had all played a part in their decision to come back 'home'. Like so many Brits, they had moved their belongings and their bodies to this place, but their hearts were still based in Southampton.

They had been comfortable, he supposed, on the shores of the Mediterranean, never wealthy but not poor either. He had gathered work around a customer base and used the British community out there as a platform, and had gained almost a monopoly in that niche market. He could offer financial deals connected to British companies that were normally not available without a lot of work by the customer. But as Kenneth and his wife were both getting older, life was also getting harder, and comfort - both emotional and physical - harder to achieve.

The summers were getting to the point where the heat was hard to take. They sat most of the day in their air-conditioned lounge, especially during August, not only because of the heat - the sun was constant day after day - but because of the tourists, particularly the French who drove Kenneth to distraction. They were so close to the border with France; it was a mere day trip for any French people living south of Toulouse, and they came in their droves, to eat, drink and buy stuff cheaply. In latter years, the 'buy cheaply' had become more of a myth than a reality, with prices in Catalunya catching up with those in France. The passing of August was always a relief; they got their area back somewhat and the expat British groups started to meet again. The main thing for Kenneth was that they could look forward to some cooler nights. But then in the distance was the other extreme: the winter. The Tramontana, the wind that blew for days, bringing icy cold draughts down from the snow-covered Pyrenees, could drive a person insane. This agony, for that was how Kenneth viewed it, was tempered with the pure visual beauty of the mountains plainly visible from their terrace and on sunny clear days the view could be breathtaking. The pure white-capped mountains seemed to illuminate themselves as they stood out against a rich blue sky. Sometimes it was bizarre to see all that snow when the sun was shining offering some winter warmth, but as soon as the sun lost its ability to comfortably warm with its rays, the cold would set in and could often bring with it that damnable wind again. It was said locally that the wind could drive a man crazy, and Kenneth could well understand that: there was no escape from it - even indoors you could hear that roar: it didn't go away. As they got older they were less able to cope with these extremes that summer and winter threw at them.

Helen had become increasingly unwell. The trouble was that nobody was ever quite sure from what she was suffering, but suffering she was, or so it seemed to those that surrounded her. The symptoms were lethargy and allegedly not being able to move a lot, which resulted in weight being loaded onto her frame in a most unhealthy way. When she got a cough, it was a major event and she was pronounced officially sick, worthy of a mention on the increasingly long sick report that the Chairman of the British Society delivered to the monthly dinner club of fellow Brits. There would always be a sympathetic murmur, but always surpassed by some more extreme illnesses in other members and even a reported death of some poor soul who had not been seen for months but was still deeply cherished at that precise point in time.

At these lunch events, wine would flow at a rate described by even the most liberal of health advisers as decidedly unhealthy. Even amongst the drinkers, one could pick out the 'class' drinkers, the ones that were going to have what they termed a good time, and their eyes would be able to see two corners of the restaurant at the same time. These drinkers would have an opinion on everything and so it was best not to get into conversations of a contentious nature. Kenneth always took a neutral stance, understanding that this gathering was a fertile place to obtain trade, so he usually agreed with the last person he spoke with, that way he upset nobody and thus no potential customer was offended.

Kenneth had used his undoubted sales patter in a second planning meeting of the group. He was concerned and probably – if truth were known – he expressed the views of the others.

"Look, I am a bit worried about our ambitions here," he had started addressing the others.

"There are quite serious implications taking the ferry outside of territorial waters, you know. I mean we could encounter the French Navy, let alone our own. And what happens when we get there? We would need to take food and provisions, not just for ourselves but for the other people onboard."

He had made a point. And others added to it.

"We should also have some consideration for the others you know – I mean they may be crossing for an appointment at QA hospital, or going for a job interview or something." piped in Kenneth's good friend, Ken.

"Yeah, some people may have waited weeks or months for an appointment. I mean you imagine if you've got really bad piles or something even worse," added Sarah.

Joyce winced and wondered why she had to bring up something like that. Why couldn't it be something like a hip replacement? That's what most old people seemed to need.

"Mm, I do see what you mean." Hardy was both disappointed and relieved in a way but could see the reality of the comments.

"Perhaps we just get them to drive round the Harbour or along the beaches with a banner or something."

"Wow, that's much more realistic," said Ollie.

The group agreed the new action: there had been little discussion and all of them seemed relieved that a more realistic approach was being taken.

Whilst in Spain, Kenneth always drove a UK-registered car, a rather old and large Range Rover. This was his link with home. He never acknowledged it but it was another way of saying to the locals that he was from the UK. In some way, that was important; it linked him to his original tribe. For years he loved life in Catalunya. Initially he did not believe that going back to the UK would improve his life at all, or come to that, that of his wife. She received constant attention from the CATSALUT, the medical organisation in the area. They looked after her very well, and from the things he had heard about the NHS back home, he doubted that such care would be lavished on her. Indeed, many of the stories bandied around in the alcohol-fuelled discussions seemed to confirm that, and he was assured that the health service in Catalunya was a country mile superior to that in the UK. In fact, he thought it was a 'forever' subject matter, always being raised, always the prejudices that the NHS was being run into the ground by foreigners who had paid nothing into it. Kenneth always thought that an irony when considering that the Brits were doing exactly the same thing in Catalunya. It was though, to most of the Brits, who were retired and ageing, a most important subject.

In common with many pensioners, not just in Europe or England, most of those over sixty were already in receipt of some sort of ongoing medical assistance. The Brits would moan; they thought on behalf of the locals that the medical centres were full of pregnant Muslims. It was true that the relationship to local women versus incoming populations seemed heavily in favour of Muslim women, but Kenneth would sometimes argue that those women were more easily identifiable than say an Irish or British woman. It was easy for the Brits to believe that every health service in the world was better than the NHS.

But the problem for Kenneth – no, it wasn't a problem he thought, it was more of an unease - he always felt slightly out of it. He had thought he had integrated, but not so. His wife had pointed out to him that if you did not speak the language of the country you were choosing to live in, then you would always be on the periphery of that community. Every so often that exclusion would show.

Kenneth's brother lived in England; Kenneth and Helen had a daughter and son, also in England, and two grandchildren, who every time he saw them, stared at this creature from some place elsewhere, far away. It always took a couple of hours to establish who he was. The 'kids' seldom came down to Catalunya. It had started off OK, down most summers, but then they wanted to use their holidays to go to other places. Mum and Dad came second, if at all. Why wouldn't they? It was Mum and Dad who had taken the decision to move miles away, which could be interpreted as being uninterested in family. It had been 'Mum and Dad' who had decided to 'run away', as the family saw it and to separate themselves from the others in search of that something or other, which people seem to need to do every so often in their life.

Added to several other issues they decided to sell up in Catalunya. They had just felt the need to return to the UK: not so much logic, just a feeling. In the tradition of leavers, they kept it secret. That's what people did down here Kenneth felt. If they had said they were going back, the remaining months would be hard; one would have been left out of the social circle because there was no long-term friendship available, and so not worth nurturing, so it was kept a secret. It was not a secret for long - it took just three days before the house was seen in one of the estate agent's windows, and the phone started ringing.

"Just testing the market," he would say, "Nothing behind it really, but we'll see what happens." The remark convinced nobody - everyone immediately knew what was really going on.

The usual professional buyers appeared along with the odd 'wheel kicker'. Kenneth had been convinced that the agents actually hired people posing as potential buyers, so it looked like the agent was 'doing the business'. They were mainly French people, who grunted appropriately at every juncture. They seemed poker faced and never gave a thing away, but one of them eventually made an offer. It was ridiculously low, and Kenneth took the view that they were, as he termed it, taking the piss. He would hold out for more, but they didn't come back. He went into his agent.

"That's all it's worth," she told him. Not wrapped up in sugar-coated language at all, just the plain ugly truth.

He remembered that sinking feeling, realising that the market in the UK had stormed ahead while there was a severe over-supply in Spain, a double whammy so to speak. The Spanish had built houses and apartments like crazy for years, always aware that the value the following year would be more than this year, but now it was the other way round. The banking crisis, along with general stupid laws on taxation made by the government, meant that interest in buying in Spain had died almost completely. Many Spanish people were unable to pay their mortgage and the banks had repossessed lots and lots of property. The result of this was that the banks had become the biggest estate agents in the country, and the effect was that they depressed the market by merely wishing to cover their own debt rather than asking market price. Bastards, thought Kenneth. Their timing was terrible.

Kenneth and Helen toyed with the idea of letting the property but unfortunately so was everyone else who couldn't sell. The 'casa', the house, became a different place now. Because they couldn't escape, it became a prison and Spain became the prison yard where they exercised and met others.

Kenneth's mental health was not helped when he was pulled over by the Mossos, the Catalan police. He was, to be fair, a target because with UK plates on his car, sailing around the place all the time, he was instantly recognisable. The police wanted to know how long he had lived there and why the car was not registered in Girona. They insisted he should have registered it some time ago; if he failed to register the car in the next seven days, they would confiscate it.

The car incident had the effect of driving both Kenneth and his – now very large – wife into a form of depression. Their lives were covered in a black shroud. The sun, whilst shining in the sky, brought little light into their world now. Kenneth mused on the irony that the thing that could cheer and give so much pleasure meant little unless the inner self was at peace. There seemed no way out of this conundrum.

But as a financial advisor he should be able to solve this, he thought. He decided he could sort out money - enough to get back to the UK and buy a small property until he could sell up in Spain.

So Kenneth embarked on a process that took him not outside the law exactly, but not within it either. At least he had joined most others in Spain, he thought, who all seemed to have dodgy pasts.

He set about re mortgaging their Spanish house at a level which was highly speculative. He filled in the forms himself, got the survey done by a mate and within two months they had money in their hands in the form of an equity release from a finance house in the UK.

It had not taken long to re-acclimatise themselves to the UK. The dark skies almost seemed reassuring, the shops were open all day, the people behind the counters actually seemed to want to help, and the estate agents were obliging. But then they remembered that the UK observed laws … and they were asked where they had got their money from. Kenneth lied; he told them it was savings, a lifetime of savings, and that they were letting the house in Spain. Kenneth was still not sure whether he had broken the law, and if he had, did anyone actually care?

The houses they saw were dingy, small and uninspiring. The roads were grey and often the wheely bins would be scattered over the pavements, along with odd bits of rubbish left over from the emptying. A fox would dart out in front of them and stare, quite confident that it could make a getaway if challenged. The odd cheap lager can tinkled as the breeze drove it further from its landing point. But then the sun came out, for just a few minutes, and everyone and everything changed, grateful for the light. The sun did raise the mood but the houses were still small. Some smelt of dog, some even worse smelt of wet dog. They were being sent to 'doer uppers', which nowadays was not really their bag. Physically, let alone emotionally, neither of them felt they could deal with anything like major building works or alterations. About the most Kenneth thought he could cope with now were some minor decorating tasks.

The areas were also suspect, in their opinion. They were not overly enthusiastic about living alongside young families. Noise, vandalism and even the fear of violence from younger people were traits they would rather avoid. In fact Kenneth was beginning to think that perhaps they should be looking at some retirement village - that would solve no end of their problems.

He did. He then dismissed it due to the cost of the original purchase and the ongoing service charges. Any company that ran these schemes have you caught by the short and curlies, he would tell Helen, with the ability to pile on costs at any time and with little scrutiny as to where funds would end up. But one thing was clear.

"It's our price range. That is the problem, I guess," Kenneth told Helen, who was returning to depression after the lift of thinking they had escaped. "If we had more money, then we would be seeing better houses." They were staying with Kenneth's brother, who lived in Lee-on-the-Solent. Kenneth and his wife were both taken by the area where his brother lived. They had landed back into the UK on the car ferry, disembarking at the Portsmouth Harbour terminal. They had made a quick decision to stay in that area, mainly because they had Kenneth's brother there, but also they were attracted by the area with its vast and varied coastline.

What should have been fun, house-hunting, was turning into a chore. It needed a piece of luck, and that came in the shape of a phone call from their agent in Spain. At long last they had achieved an offer on the house that Kenneth felt they could accept. It was so much money, but they would have to pay back the mortgage equity advance, which of course reduced the sum they would actually achieve.

Kenneth and Helen told the estate agent in the UK that they were not finding what they wanted in the price range they had given, so the agent started sending them to more expensive houses. These were better, much better, houses with views of the Solent, or Portsmouth Harbour, houses where they could sit and just stare at the charming view, sipping a gin and tonic, and whiling away the hours in peace.

The process of selling a house in Spain is quite different to the adversarial process in England. Kenneth knew that it took months to actually register a charge on a property in Spain: the paperwork, although diligently done by the lenders in the UK, could take months to be processed, and Kenneth took advantage of that. As far as the equivalent to the Land Registry in Spain was concerned, no charges appeared on the system. Kenneth and his wife could walk away with the money. A chasm opened up before them. Not his fault, he convinced himself, but that of the system in Spain, which never picked up the fact that there was a charge on the place. So, by transferring the guilt to someone else, Kenneth felt more justified and less guilty.

The transaction was traditional, with all parties seated round a table. Kenneth's agent turned up with the paperwork. She sat there, slim, with black hair and thick horn-rimmed glasses, bursting with high-end fashion which indicated money, and of course she was getting some more from him. She spoke French, Catalan, Spanish and quite good English. Kenneth spoke only English and enough

Spanish to order drinks, meals and pay bills. She made him feel slightly inadequate because he had to rely on her to explain what was going on.

The buyers sat opposite him, a young couple embarking on their first purchase. The couple were happy, with a fantastic life ahead of them. They kept gazing at one another, so obviously in love. They had their agent / solicitor with them as well as their bank manager.

The 'Notario', the man with the power, sat at the end of the table. He was very pleasant and smiled. Catalan men can smile whilst knifing you, thought Kenneth.

He spoke English and did so for the benefit of Kenneth and his wife.

Hurdle one: "I of course need to check your identification, so perhaps you could show me your passports please."

The number on the passport did not match the number on the documents they had produced when they had bought the property. The reason was that, when Brits got a new passport, the number changed.

"I need then to photocopy this passport. Why do the Brits do everything in an awkward way? You drive on the other side the road, you use a different currency, you guard your border against your friends but let in terrorists. I have a job understanding you sometimes."

He got away with it because he said this with a smile, and to be blunt Kenneth could not argue with much of what the man had said anyway. Living in Spain, or indeed anywhere abroad, one got the chance to look back at the dear old home country, and one became aware of, let's say, its peculiarities.

The 'sale' meeting was all very amicable, with the bank giving over a cheque for the full payment for the property.

Kenneth immediately placed the cheque in his pocket, handed over the keys and 'legged it'.

Within one hour they were driving across the border into France and heading towards the channel ports. Even in these circumstances, there was some sadness saying goodbye to the Mediterranean. In France, past Perpignan, there was a turn to the left that took you dramatically away from the views of the sea, and you started the journey north to Toulouse, past the walled city of Carcassonne after which you started to lose the terrain of the Med. It was a long drive to the English Channel, and a long time to be together in the car, and a long time to think.

The money he had just received went to his head, and he used all of it to purchase a nice property in Lee-on-the-Solent. It took several months before the mortgagees of his Spanish property found him. His forwarding address had been not exactly fictitious, but it should have been. He had, at the last knockings in Spain, given the address where he grew up in Southampton. The current occupiers had bought the house from Kenneth's mother when she had been taken into a care home and they were able to refer the mortgagees to the home and - even after so many years - they were able to trace where her funds had been held. After the appropriate authorities had gone through all the obstacles of data protection, they had been given permission by the courts to go on a 'fishing trip' in as much as they asked that same bank if the had an account relating to Kenneth. Of course there was, and indeed Kenneth had paid his mother's fees from his bank account. He was now being pursued by the mortgagees of the property in Spain. Kenneth knew the letter was coming - it had to - and to some degree it was almost a relief when it dropped through the letterbox onto their expensive door mat. The letter was courteous enough, and merely reminded Kenneth and his wife of the agreement they had entered into to refund any advance made to them from the proceeds of any sale. But the last bit of the communication was not quite as nice.

"Without further investigation, there would appear to be a deliberate attempt to defraud the company, which of course we take very seriously. We would welcome your comments on this matter and also demand repayment of the sum involved along with consequential expenses."

Kenneth did not like this current situation. It had taken over eight months to catch up with him and even then the company was treading carefully, making doubly sure they had their man and that any underlying threats were couched in reasonableness. But they did have him, he knew that, and he became bitter again.

There were few people he could share his story with to lighten the load, but he did talk to Ken, his new-found friend who he believed he could trust.

"There's was no way I can return the money," he told Ken,

"What about selling? You would still have enough equity to get something else," Ken proposed.

"That would be the final straw for Helen, and probably kill her. On top of that, the company's not far from referring the matter to their solicitors to investigate grounds of criminal fraud."

Ken reflected silently now on the seriousness of his friend's predicament, not really able to contribute much.

"I suppose a new equity release scheme is out of the question at the moment," Ken ventured. The remark was met with just an expression from Kenneth, which indicated that the 'out of the question' bit was indeed correct.

Kenneth had not bothered his wife with any of this,

believing even at this stage that somehow the matter would just go away. He still felt hard done by and that the world had conspired against him. How come those with money could get away with such things? How come people like 'Fred the Shred' could get millions for screwing up a bank, still live the high life in a castle in Scotland? Yet Kenneth would no doubt be imprisoned, his wife made homeless and dying without him. They would be left at the foot of the hill when it came to state support, even though they had spent years paying in for it. From that bitterness stemmed much more bitterness. The whole world was against him, and then he thought - no, not just him; he could join with others who also felt the world was against them.

He had over the months grown tired. It was then that he saw an advertisement in the paper that proclaimed a 'Spanish culture' group that met in Gosport's brilliant and vibrant Discovery Centre, a library by any other name. He wondered whether there would be others there that had encountered anything like he had and so he went along.

At least this group had interested him and he started to meet local people, one guy in particular by the name of Ken. At least that name was easy for him to remember!

The group, of course, welcomed a chap like Kenneth; having lived in Spain he could bring much of value to the group. They would be enchanted with his stories of Spanish officialdom and of farming methods, and his views on how millions of euros had been wasted on building empty motorways and railway stations. They were less impressed when they realised that he could speak hardly any Spanish, let alone Catalan. The group had been eagerly awaiting the time they could practise their poor Spanish with a fluent Spanish speaker but it soon became obvious that their wait was going to continue. Kenneth was still very welcome.

Of course, there was no one in the group that had anything like his problems, or indeed would even understand it. The solution was that he either had to come up with the money to pay the company back, or they would repossess his current home. The realisation hit him that this situation was of his own making: no one else could be blamed, and no one else was going to get him out of it. Even if he found the money, there was nothing to say they would still not seek judicial justice regarding the fraud element.

He had, he thought, one last gasp. The house they lived in now was unencumbered, bought with cash. He could and should be able, with his contacts, to arrange an equity release on that one, enough to settle the bill with the first company and thus be left in peace. He would, he resolved, try that one, providing of course he wasn't on any sort of blacklist yet. The only other issue would be that his wife would need to be a joint signatory, and that would mean coming clean that they had been found out, not something that he was looking forward to.

What this dubious action on the Gosport Ferry was going to achieve remained to be seen, but at this moment, Kenneth sat in this dingy railway station with a rather suspect cup of coffee in front of him. He was not convinced that anything of any use would come out of it. Indeed, it might even get him into more trouble with the authorities, but for the next few hours at least, it was a distraction from his problems on the home front.

This whole business with the loans, or some may even call it theft, had aged him. He disliked looking in the mirror now and his facial appearance had not escaped others.

"Are you OK?" asked his friend Ken.

"Sure, never better," Kenneth replied.

Ken had not been convinced and pursued it in a not overtly diplomatic nature.

"Well, I've got to say you don't look well, and you seem a bit distant to me. I mean if it's something I've said, you need to be out with it. Or is there some medical problem?"

"You're right, I don't look well, Ken. I saw myself in the mirror this morning, but I think it's just that I am tired. Helen keeps me up most of the night, night after night. She tells me her pain is worse than ever, in every joint she says, and the problem is that there seems little one can do about it."

Ken seemed more satisfied with that; he was understanding and knew the burden that his friend Kenneth was carrying.

"Well, if there's anything I can do to help, just let me know won't you?"

Kenneth was touched by that, but of course there was not a lot unless he could stump up thousands of pounds.

Kenneth had continued to try and muster business on his return to the UK but much had changed. He was not a 'legal' financial advisor for a start; he had never done any of the exams that needed to be taken nowadays in order to call yourself a financial advisor. He had few connections in the Gosport area, where if you were ex-forces it was like having contacts in one of the biggest clubs going. But as he was neither, there was not much to go and work on there, and even if he did he would be outside the law.

"Well, no change there then," Helen had spitefully said to him.

"Look, I had to do this stuff, it's no good you getting mad now. You went along with it, you knew everything."

She just looked at him: she had gone along with it and what she had just said was unfair.

She smiled and said, "Sorry, that was unnecessary."

Her smile continued. He looked at her, now ageing, now obese, now disabled, but in those seconds age dropped away from her and there was love in her watery eyes. She had hurt the man that was caring for her and had cared for her all these years and that was not fair. Even though what she had said was true, sometimes the truth was best left unsaid. He could just see that wonderful blonde woman he had married nearly fifty years ago; she was still there under the ravaged skin and flesh that hung without distinction, constantly reminding others that she was ageing.

He leant across their table and kissed her. He placed one hand on the leaf of the cheap table they had bought for the kitchen in order to steady himself. The table collapsed, their tea spilling onto the floor, one cup breaking, sugar going everywhere, and it was luck that he didn't follow it all, as God withdrew the support of the kitchen table from his arm.

"Oh blinking hell," was his response

She looked, and smiled again and then laughed.

"Kenneth, I love you," she said. That was so precious a thing to tell him after all these years and after all they had been through, and were actually going through now. Kenneth wondered if her repose would be the same if she knew the position they were actually in. His fear was a court bailiff knocking the door when she as alone in the house to deal with it. She would not know what was going on and he feared her reaction and the consequences.

Helen had hit it off straight away after she had been introduced to Sarah, Ken's 'friend'. The relationship between all four was an instant success, even though it reminded Kenneth of friendships formed in Spain with Brits that promised you friendship for life, then would be gone to the next set of friends until your turn came round again. They would then spend the first couple of hours with you slagging off the very people they had pushed you away for, so Kenneth was a little cautious with Ken and Sarah at first. But this relationship did seem for 'keeps'. The idea of a day of adventure with them appealed to Kenneth, and Helen had assured him that she would be fine until around five o'clock.

Ken and Sarah had also introduced Kenneth and Helen to their church friends. This had been important because for various reasons Ken and Sarah were under some sort of moral scrutiny from the church mafia. Were they having an affair? Heaven forbid. To introduce new people to the church was a feather in the cap for them, although Ken held out little hope of Helen and Kenneth becoming church members.

Now, sitting in the cafe, the issues played on Kenneth's mind, as did the possibility that today might just be the day a court bailiff arrived on the doorstep. It also worried him a bit that other people were noticing the physical effects the whole thing was having on him. He must have really aged in just a few weeks for people to notice like that. It was also a bit of an eye opener, in as much that he had never really subscribed to the theory that worry could manifest itself in the face of the individual. It looked like, and felt like, he might have to rethink that.

CHAPTER 5

"Why? What do you mean we can't do it travelling back?" said Olly

"Well, all the plans were for doing it travelling from Gosport to Portsmouth – I just can't do things going backwards." Hardy had been flustered by the question.

"We've also tried to arrange the press coverage and that needs to be done on the Portsmouth side."

That response, however, confused and angered Olly. He wanted to just get on with it, he wanted it over. Kenneth was getting more and more anxious as it was getting late, and this would add at least another three quarters of an hour before the venture could begin in earnest. He wanted to be back home with his wife.

The day was getting hotter. Bert was suffering from both the heat and having to carry the banner around. His brow carried beads of sweat which threatened to run down behind his glasses and into his sorrowful eyes. He plainly was not enjoying this and the stress was beginning to give him heartburn. The black coffee was not helping in that direction either.

"Had we better split up and go over in several different groups, otherwise they are going to become suspicious?" This was a good point that Ken had raised previously, or he thought he had, but obviously it had not been universally appreciated.

"Oh, for God's sake, at this rate we will be messing around for the whole day. If we split up, then that's another half hour, and we still got to re-embark the ferry as a group when we come back." Kenneth was getting frustrated now. "I have to have this done by four o'clock, I've told you that before - I can't leave my Helen on her own for any longer."

"You've not really got the hang of this, have you Kenneth?" Hardy asked what was an almost rhetorical question.

"We are meant to be making a statement, you know -you cant just put a time limit on it."

"Look, come on everyone, let's not fall out," said Sarah; often she poured oil on troubled water. "We could all go back on the same ferry but mix up with the other passengers. They will never notice us as a group, just split up that's all."

This seemed a perfectly sensible idea and one that everyone could agree on. So one by one they threaded out of the station. The air was really balmy now and the brightness was blinding; the light showed in silvery threads on the deep rich green sea that was now refilling the harbour.

The tide was still out but visibly re-entering its domain to which it was entitled, and would have it back to be sure. The aroma in the air was that of drying seaweed, and flies busied themselves flying from one piece to another seemingly having a great time. The mud was dull but probably less polluted now than it has been in years.

Bert could remember the 'mud larks', when just after the war kids would wade in the mud, beckoning to passengers from the ferry to throw odd change down to them. Lots of passengers would pause their journey just to watch the boys wallow in the mud to find the coins, and it became a source of amusement for many passengers. Bert had known several of the boys but never got involved. There was quite a nasty side to it because there was a real pecking order on who got most of the money, which could amount to as much as ten shillings a week, quite a sum in those days. The 'seniority' and the tribal order – Portsmouth boys versus Gosport boys – often spilt over into violence, and protection money was often required.

The *Warrior*, one of the first iron-clad ships, bathed in the warm water and sun, fluttering her flags dressed overall. People queued on the jetty waiting to board her, others queued further along waiting for the next boat tour of the harbour. Children ran in and out of adults, shouting and squealing, and of course the compulsory beggar, still homeless, still starving, spread across the pavement waiting for a contribution to his funds.

Taxis waiting for customers; everywhere, people were waiting for something. And now, people filed onto the jetty waiting for the ferry to return from Gosport.

Hardy and Joyce preferred to stay as a couple. They were a couple after all, and there was nothing suspicious in that. They wandered down the pontoon, now going steeply downhill. Workman were painting the posts that held the train station above the sea. They had to do it now when the tide was out, and whilst one could hear them, shouting and singing sometimes, Hardy could never actually see them.

The green-and-white vessel was moving from Gosport pontoon, churning a white tail as she nosed across the harbour. She went up-harbour slightly to avoid an outgoing yacht, and then dived outwards to avoid an incoming Border Force unit. Years of practice gave an excellent safety record to the ferry service, with collisions practically unheard of.

Hardy and Joyce ignored their friends and for a little while they were actually a couple again. Not speaking of course: not because there was nothing to say, but because of the passively aggressive non-verbal protest being mounted by Joyce. True to the arrangements, the others had scattered themselves amongst the queue. There must have only been thirty or so other souls waiting, but it was sufficient number to camouflage the group. This was going to plan and they would all meet again in the delightful Falkland Gardens on benches looking out to the harbour on the Gosport side.

Joyce and Hardy sat to the rear of the ferry; they were on their own as they made their way back over to Gosport. It was more noisy back there, so even if he wanted to talk, Hardy would have had to shout and he couldn't be bothered to do that. So he sat, staring at the sea, and questioned why he was doing this.

Hardy

Hardy had run his own specialist sports-car repair workshop. He had learnt his trade in a decent enough way in the RAF, repairing engines and ground vehicles. He raced motorbikes around the lanes of Sussex years ago, and all in all had been a thorough nuisance to the community around the area. His business had flourished, however, mainly because he was cheaper than the dealers, but as engines and maintenance routines became more sophisticated, the business had started to suffer. Car manufacturers built cars with specific tool kits and diagnostic machines which were very expensive to buy, giving - quite deliberately - a competitive advantage to the dealership franchises. The idea had been to sell the business on at some date, and make enough money out of it to invest in a decent pension, but it hadn't worked out like that, because the value of the business had gradually decreased. When it came to selling it, nobody really wanted it, and so his pension fund was virtually non-existent. Joyce had worked as his secretary / office woman during the heyday, but seeing what was happening to the business she had taken another job as well during the last years.

Their great sadness in life, he had been told by Joyce, was they never had children.

"Just never happened," they would both tell people. Joyce claimed that she did not want any of the little brats anyway and that life was better without them. That was a cover story, however, because inside the marriage the issue had become obsessional. Joyce was so convinced it was Hardy's issue, and that perhaps he was 'firing blanks'. She had insisted on him being tested and he had duly supplied a sample of his 'ammunition' which, as it happened, turned out to be normal. The tests had been carried out in the Royal Naval Hospital Haslar, which sat on a promontory coast in Gosport. He had been surprised to be sent there, thinking they only dealt with service personnel; he had also been surprised that they had sent him into a cubicle to provide his sample, with some porn magazines. Very down-to-earth, he had thought. Whilst embarrassing at the time, the tests had changed the landscape of their marriage considerably, giving Hardy in his own mind greater masculinity after several years of 'her' challenging it. He was normal.

Of course, the retrieval of his manhood had not been achieved easily; he was aware that she had tried to become pregnant by another guy during the whole process, and whilst on the outside he had accepted this and just got on with life, it had, deep down it had hurt him very much. He remembered the night - he could never forget it - and he had lain in bed sobbing uncontrollably from midnight until he heard her return at around half past three, or it could have been as late as four. He did, however, know her well enough to know how to get to her, and it was vital that he showed no concern whatsoever. He was able to keep his back to her, pretending to be asleep, despite her making as much noise as possible when she undressed and put clothes away. He knew it was done to try and wake him but he was not going to give her that satisfaction. He could feel her fury as she climbed in beside him.

The results of the tests created strange behaviour in Joyce. She could not point her accusatory finger any more and that provoked her into being even more aggressive towards Hardy, which to this very day he still suffered from. In the past few years they had become acutely aware of a 'missing family', particularly around times like Christmas and other holidays. They lavished presents on their nephews and nieces, of whom - as they got older - they seemed to see less and less. Of course that might have had something to do with the fact that Joyce was currently not talking to her sister, the result of a row over a timeshare they all had in Malaga.

A side-effect of not having children was that there was a major gap in conversation areas. While other people would relate how well their eldest son was doing, or that their grandchildren were on their way to university, Hardy and Joyce had to content themselves with nods of approval, and by changing subjects to outrageous politics or the wine they had at the restaurant the other lunchtime. Both Hardy and Joyce would become bored listening to others going on and on about their offspring. Hardy would even say to Joyce that there was nothing more boring than hearing about other people's holidays, or how wonderfully their kids or grandchildren were succeeding. You seldom heard of the children failing, seldom did you hear that the grandchild was a drug dealer or a prostitute operating in the back streets of Slough: to do so would be refreshing, he thought.

They lived with the situation now; there was frankly no choice, and age dictated that it was way beyond the point of doing anything about it anyway. Now in their early seventies they would not even be candidates for adopting anyone and they certainly did not want the problems of fostering. They had looked into it once before and Joyce had not been impressed, saying that all the products on offer had been in her own words, "badly soiled." Every child offered by Social Services had problems and so the idea had petered out. Again Hardy had been bemused as to what Joyce had expected. Was the clue not in the term 'Social Services?' he had wondered.

However, asked if they had a happy marriage, he would expect doubts to be expressed on both sides. They had had their moments, and sometimes they had periods of rejuvenating the marriage. Hardy had supposed when he married Joyce that it would be a conventional happy-ever-after type of affair but the marriage had never been that. Joyce had been volatile from day one: indeed, in his opinion, she had behaved in the worst way she ever could have done on their wedding night - she had spent most of the evening dancing with a former male work colleague of hers. She had admitted at the time that she fancied him, but many of the guests had been quite opinionated about the way she had danced with him, leaving her brand new husband, somewhat embarrassed, on the sidelines. It was a bit obvious to all that she was what Hardy referred to as dancing on her ex-boss' leg, no doubt achieving some sort of sexual gratification out of it. Her arms were wrapped around his shoulders and Hardy thought he detected a note of embarrassment from her ex-boss - even he was finding this a bit too much. "A bit too intimate." was the popular opinion. At least she went off with Hardy when it was time to retire but, as she had made it absolutely clear to him, she was far too tired for sex.

She explained to Hardy that it was better for both of them to wait until she was ripe for taking and could devote all her energy into it; that way he and she would enjoy it better. It was, thought Hardy, no real big deal that there was to be no sex on his wedding night. In common with many couples who married in the sixties and seventies, they had not waited for the marriage ceremony to consummate their relationship, and indeed she had not been a virgin either. He could say nothing about that as he had lost his virginity to a prostitute in London six weeks after he had been called up for National Service. To say that he had enjoyed it would have been wrong; the woman demanded extra to take her top off, extra to kiss him, extra to obtain entry from behind which had been his fantasy. In fact it he likened it to buying a car whereby in those days it seemed that even the wheels were sold as an optional extra. He had felt 'seen off' as a result, and left feeling sullied, robbed of twenty quid, and had lost his belt as well as his virginity. He had been with a group of other lads but he had not felt the urge to talk about the experience, feeling pretty much undone by the whole event. The woman, or prostitute – and both were correct – made no attempt at all to disguise the fact that this was no more than a money-making exercise on her behalf.

In turn, back in the sixties, there seemed to be two types of people: those who could loosely be expressed as 'enjoying' themselves, and those that were not. He was meant to be on the 'enjoying' side, being in the RAF, but it appeared to him that the real enjoyment was coming from those attending clubs and trendy bars, using drugs, and rocking and rolling until the early hours. Apparently sex was freely available from mini-skirted young things that walked around in a state of semi-narcosis, but Hardy could never quite get his hands on them. He had thought he should demonstrate against the war in Vietnam: there were loads of heady flower-power girls expressing their disagreement, as there were later at Greenham Common. But that became a bit tricky being in the Royal Air Force. He would be immediately sticking out like a sore thumb - he had short hair for heaven's sake, while now all the boys followed the examples set by the likes of the Beatles and Rolling Stones.

He actually found life easier when he left the RAF and started his business, and indeed started his first serious relationship. He had achieved the odd 'fumble' from NAAFI dances, but nothing of what he would call 'note'.

The pontoon had started rocking, bringing Hardy back to the real world from his day-dreaming and reminiscing. A large cross-Channel ferry had just passed on its way to France, and the wake was now moving the pontoon in such a manner that he actually felt a little bit woozy. Joyce put her hand out to steady herself, clutching at Hardy's arm. The action of the outstretched arm reinforced his earlier comments to her that her three-inch stiletto heels were indeed not the kit for such a day's action As usual, she had taken no notice of his warnings. At that moment Hardy would have give his eye teeth to see her rolling across the pontoon floor in an inelegant manner. But fun like that just didn't happen to him any more.

He started repairing cars, visiting people on their driveway, where he achieved experience not only on the Ford Anglia and the Austin Mini, but with the occasional wife. Sometimes bored and loose of morality, they would invite him in for 'coffee'. He had learned about the joint oil and petrol pump on old Ford Consuls, and he had learned where the starter buttons were on the mark one female.

The business took off; there was an obvious need for a 'cheap' mechanic and he was able to rent a small but adequate workshop. It wasn't long before he realised that paperwork played as much a part in his life as did spanners. He needed help. And then; then there was Joyce. She organised him and almost took over his life within two weeks. Paperwork dated some nine months previously was prioritised and dealt with, and most of all, the phone was answered. Work piled in. But there was more to this than just being a secretary. She was hot. Long legs, blonde with brains, too good to give up, and so, the relationship started.

The saving grace for Joyce was that she was a fantastic lover when eventually turned on and let go, a far cry from the old experienced prostitute he had encountered in London. In fact as he got older, her energy and passion had become too much sometimes.

In the last ten years or so, both Joyce and Hardy had both largely lost interest in sex. He did his best to maintain it, by invoking various fantasies that he had developed over the years, but these fantasies were in his head; he seldom discussed any of them with Joyce for fear of a withering tongue-lashing.

Hardy was also aware that his failure to sell the business had left them in financial difficulties, and that the lifestyle he had offered Joyce early on in life was not now available.

They had downsized when moving to Gosport and the house was not something that Joyce was tremendously proud to invite her friends to. They did little entertaining, and now their social life revolved around the church mainly, which didn't exactly excite Hardy. He often asked himself whether he was an 'attendee' at church for the right reasons. Take the church away and their social life practically disappeared. That should not be the reason to attend church, he would reason. He had long since taken the view that religion in its raw state was a leftover from a very effective way of controlling the peasant. The tool and concept of a glorious afterlife, providing you toed the line on this planet, was still effectively used by several religions.

But to Hardy, lots of the teachings made sense, in as much as the Ten Commandments were the perfect set of rules for living together on this planet. The problem was that many of these rules seemed to apply only to certain sections of society. For those people, those that seemed to matter, the rules were only applied when it was convenient. The hypocrisy made him cross sometimes. When he thought these issues through, it made him cross that nobody really took any notice of his views anyway: not Joyce, not his brother or nephews or nieces, not his MP. Come to that, did he himself even think his views were valid?

So to find himself in the role as leader of this group of rebels, Hardy was not in his comfort zone, but at least life meant something again. How quickly things can change in life! Being the self-appointed leader of this group made him fairly important and responsible. Their protest could have far-reaching repercussions. Indeed he felt somewhat like others that had gone before him: Nelson Mandela, that Pankhurst woman, and the chappy from the Polish dockyard whose name he could not quite remember.

His health was what one might call OK for his age. He had been called in for a medical when he had reached seventy and had been told all the things that most people are told - too much cholesterol, obese, inactive and drinks too much. Bugger! What joys were left in life, he asked himself, if he couldn't even have a Greggs sausage roll and a couple of glasses of red wine to wash it down?

"But you don't just have a couple of glasses do you?" Joyce had countered. "You have the whole bloody bottle, and some."

That argument was difficult, and it went into the 'too difficult' column and was ignored. He had tried going for walks, he even contemplated the gym once, but that was crazy - his nature was that he was slow at everything; every movement was almost thought-about and deliberate, nothing was instantaneous. So the gym was out.

He had tried the swimming pool, which Joyce had agreed to go to with him. The local authority pool was too cold and the private one in a hotel further out of town was far too expensive and took too much effort to get to. He had so thoroughly had not enjoyed the experience in the local authority pool: to some degree he knew why. Both he and Joyce were essentially snobs, and to share a changing room with the 'social housing' people was just too much. And then there was the guy that was trying to get Joyce to go into his cubicle with him; that was embarrassing all round and could have turned nasty. The plus side was that Joyce was in a super mood for some two hours after that event, receiving an ego boost that she had far from expected. Hardy had been unable to believe the cheek of it. It wasn't even like he was handsome or muscular, but it had obviously worked for the old geezer in the past, given his confidence. Somehow, these things just happened to Joyce.

Today Hardy was finding thinking on his feet difficult. He got confused and flustered these days, and of course the last six weeks had not helped in that.

Out of the blue, Joyce had decided she wanted a divorce after some forty years of marriage. Hardy had decided that this was an idle threat, and that it was just one more time that she had used threats and scare tactics. But what was different was that this time she was calm; this call for a divorce was not part of a row, not part of some outrageous retribution, and to a degree he felt unnerved by that.

He was even more surprised when she informed him that she had an appointment with a solicitor on Wednesday morning. She seemed to mean it this time, and he needed to think how he felt about this. This was an entirely new scenario.

The realisation that he had no one to talk to about it made him feel even worse. He could, he supposed, talk to Bert or even Ken, but in a way they were too close to Joyce as well and would probably be reluctant to get involved. In common with many men, he did not have much of a social circle, and in any case, in his view running to anyone was a sign of weakness and also very embarrassing.

In retrospect, his decision to take himself off to London on the day of her appointment was bizarre to say the least. Why, he wondered as the train started to move, was he even doing this? What was that going to achieve? The train rattled slowly out of Portsmouth Harbour station, a rather run-down shed that Railtrack had the cheek to call a station, to the central Portsmouth and Southsea station, a matter of a couple of hundred yards. His aim was to be out when Joyce got back so he didn't have to suffer her gloating. He knew that she would come back full of confidence and bluster.

A young girl got on the train at Fratton, home station to Portsmouth Football Club. She sat opposite Hardy. He guessed she was about twenty, and true to the habits of that age group it took no more than ten seconds for the inevitable mobile phone to come out. The phone seemed to fit into a hand that God had designed to hold it. The other hand presented a finger, skilled in the operation of the device. She was obviously texting. He knew the word but apart from that not a lot more. It was a tech world that he had not explored.

She then placed the phone to her ear.

"No, I never said that," she suddenly blurted out.

Hardy could hear a voice on the other end. It sounded male, and it sounded like he was not a happy male.

"Look, if you want to believe that fucking cow, that's your probs, I've had enough of you fucking about with me head. You can get stuffed, you're binned."

Hardy wondered whether he had witnessed the end of a relationship. She ceased the phone call. Would the guy ring her back? Hardy waited in anticipation but no call came. By now she had tears in her eyes. Should he say anything, he wondered? None of this was any of his business and yet in that short conversation she had involved him by talking in public and not even in a hushed manner.

Hardy took the plunge. He had, he thought, never spoken to a girl this young since he was that young, except for the odd shop assistant or teller in the bank.

"Are you alright?" he asked tentatively.

She looked across at him. To her he looked like no more than a kindly old man with soulful eyes, greying and thinning hair, slightly overweight, and offering little threat.

"Yeah, I will be in a minute." She sighed. "Sorry about that rubbish just now, but he's such a twat."

"Was that your boyfriend?" Again it was tentative, unsure of what he should be asking and what was politically correct these days. Indeed, was the term 'boyfriend' even used now? He really didn't know.

"He was. I've just binned him, haven't I?" The question was rhetorical.

There were more tears running down her cheek. Hardy couldn't help but be taken by the irony of the situation and the rather aptness of the word 'binned'.

"Bit ironic this," he decided to say after some consideration, "My wife is in the process, as we speak, of ditching me, or should I say 'binning'. She's actually at the solicitors right now."

She looked up, and now it was her turn to not know quite what to say.

"Oh my God, really?"

"Yes."

"So how long have you been married?"

"Goodness." Hardy had to think, "about forty-four years I think."

"Fucking hell, that's a long time. Why on earth are you separating now?" She asked the personal question without really thinking about it. It didn't faze Hardy, however.

"Do you know, that's a bloody good question, and I can't really give you the answer to it, because nothing was different last night, for example, than it has been for the last God-knows-how-many years. I think she just feels that enough is enough. We seldom see eye to eye and we are always arguing, and I think she would answer your question with another question as to why we didn't do this years ago."

"So just an unhappy marriage then?" she enquired, not now feeling the need to think before asking anything.

"Yes, I think you would call it that. I think she would claim it was just a habit rather than a relationship."

"Have you told your kids?"

"Ah, well there you have it, we haven't got any, and I think that has always been a source of sadness and perhaps even frustration."

"Didn't you not want any then, or was it just not to be?"

This is peculiar, thought Hardy. I am talking to this young girl who I only met five minutes ago like an old friend. How strange is that? But she is very likeable and her own problem seemed to melt away for her, so in a strange way perhaps he was even helping her as well? He continued to answer her question.

"Oh we wanted them in the beginning, in fact she became obsessed with the need. It turned out that for some medical reason, which she has never discussed with me, she was not able to conceive. She thought the problem was me at first, thought I was firing blanks. Well I tell you there was never such a big come-down as when I passed the fertility test."

"You seem sort of triumphant about that," she observed.

Hardy was a bit taken aback. He had never seen it as being triumphant, merely as getting his own back for all the jibes she had given him, and of course for the night she went with the other guy.

"Well ..." He hesitated. "I guess it is in a way, but she had put me through so much humiliation over the years we were trying for a baby. Do you know, she even went off with another guy one night, right in front of my nose, in the hope that he would make her pregnant?"

My God, he thought, he had never said anything to anyone about that, and here was this stranger listening intently to his most intimate secrets.

"Oh that's horrible," she conceded. "That must have hurt you terribly. I bet you had a right go at her, didn't you? I am surprised that you didn't throw her out there and then."

"No, no I didn't. I got to her in the way I knew best: I took no notice of her when she walked back into the room, and I never asked her a thing about it. And that made her really angry."

"I should think it did. But I get it – you thought that was the best way of hurting her. She must have thought you didn't care about her at all. I expect she still feels like that now to be honest. These little seeds planted tend to grow, don't they?"

"Oh, never looked at it like that."

"That's what me and my ex, as he is now, have fallen out about. He got told by my mate that I had gone with his best friend. It's a lie, but I swear he just wants to believe it, and if he can't believe me and prefers to believe slag offs, then there's no trust is there? No point in carrying on."

Hardy thought for a moment. He proffered a new line.

"Well …" He often started sentences with 'well' just like the young now started sentences with 'so'. "You could look at it this way: I showed so much trust in Joyce that I didn't need to question her as to where she had been until gone three in the morning without me."

"You could but you didn't, did you? But do you know they actually did anything? I mean she could have just been chilling with a film or something."

"Oh well, bit personal and sort of difficult that. I mean what else is anyone doing until gone three in the morning? And as a husband, you can tell - little things like her hair was out of its normal position, and I hope I am not going to offend you, but she changed her pants as soon as she got back, and washed herself ... if you know what I mean."

The girl could have reacted by saying that went into the realms of 'just too much information.' but she didn't. She obviously did know what he meant.

"It was her mood as well - hugely confident and happy, and she was a dream to live with again for about four weeks, until she came on again."

"But you still, to this day, don't actually know, do you? You've never asked her and to her it shows indifference and not caring."

"Yeah, course I know, but that episode didn't split us - that was over thirty years ago."

"Are you sure about that?" she asked. "Was that the period you should have both really called it a day? Deep down, it sounds to me like that was the case. It was over that night, wasn't it? I bet neither of you have actually worked on your relationship since then, and she is obviously bitter probably because in her mind you hadn't given a toss about her going off like that."

Was this girl a professional counselor, he wondered? She seemed to have insights that had never surfaced. Was it possible that he and Joyce fell out right back then?

"So, what are you doing today," she asked.

"Just getting out of it and going to London to just waste the day I suppose. I don't want to be home when she gets back, puffing her chest out and then telling me all the grisly things that are going to happen in the near future. She'll be crowing that I shall be getting a letter from her solicitor. I've got to get out of the house or something. I don't want to give her that satisfaction."

"So you're doing the same thing again to her. You are going to show that you don't give a toss about her wanting a divorce. That's what's going to come over to her. I mean, do you actually care? It may be that you are going to care about the disruption, about the changes in your life that may be difficult to cope with. Of course your wife could be right that the two of you may be happier apart."

Hardy had not thought that through at all. And to be fair, he reasoned, today was about was getting to grips with thoughts like that. He needed what was called 'space' to think things through and what his course of action might be. This young lady – where did she come from? Who or what had delivered her? She was like a light in the darkness.

With no awareness that it was happening, he found a tear running down his cheek. It was handy that the young lady had already got out tissues to sort her own tears out, and she now handed him one to mop his up.

"We're a right pair, mate, ain't we?"

In this short time, a common bond had developed. She had been lovely to him, and he appreciated that. She got off at Haslemere, too early for Hardy: he had much more to ask her but now she was gone and the seat was empty.

It was reoccupied at Woking by a man of the cloth. There was no relationship between them because the man of the cloth did not use his mobile phone. The man offered no eye contact and to be fair Hardy did not probably want it. He had had enough counselling for one day.

Hardy had not got back until quite late, past nine o'clock. He had wandered round London looking at the sights. He ate in the restaurant of his choice, which in a strange sort of way gave him a sense of freedom. He pondered going with a prostitute, but rejected it on the grounds that it would not help him at all. He had caught a train from Waterloo at nine minutes past seven. It was quiet, and he sat thinking. He had picked up a Standard but had no concentration to read much in it. The day had been eventful; in fact it had, to a large degree, done what he wanted it to do. He didn't know whether what was in his mind would work, but at least he would try when he got back home. It was going to be difficult, but he would try: in fact he would have nothing to lose.

She had the telly on when he eventually got through the door.

"Where have you been?" He was surprised at her tone: it was not angry perceptibly - there was actually an element of anxiousness in it, and did he detect relief?

"Ah, well I needed to get out of it, to get out of here and to get my head around what you are doing."

"So where have you been?"

"Well, honestly Joyce, you have rather lost the initiative by asking that question haven't you? I mean, I am gone, aren't I?"

"So you may be and you can do what you like when I don't have to take some sort of responsibility for you. You could have been taken ill or anything, I didn't know, did I?"

Within seconds, this was already going wrong. It was getting like a game of tennis again with each one of them trying to score a winning shot, the only difference being there was no umpire to mark up the score. Hardy was prepared to put a stop to it at the real risk of a major put-down. If that happened - so be it; he would still be in no worse a position than he was now.

"As I said, it is only fair that I should have time to think. I took today to do that, and I have to say your decision to go for a divorce has made me very sad."

He left a gap deliberately. She didn't respond so he went on.

"I may have not been a good husband but I have never done anything to deliberately hurt you and to be fair, Joyce, that is not how you have treated me. That night you went off with that bloke, I cried myself to sleep. I was so upset, so I may as well tell you now, I had never felt so down."

She looked up at him.

"I find that hard to believe," she replied, "You didn't seem to give a monkey's, and in any case how do you know I wasn't watching a film or something at his place?"

Hardy left that one but remembered the words of the girl on the train.

"Well you are wrong, I did care and I still do, I was devastated. I also want to say that I am so sad that our almost lifelong relationship is ending this way in recriminations and what will surely be a whole load of nastiness, because the adversarial system of divorce in this country creates that. I know we argue, I know you are contemptuous of me, I know I am not the man you married, but I am still in here."

He stopped and again there was a silence. It was a heavy silence filled with drama, Hardy thought.

"Well …" She hesitated. "Look Hardy, I thought I would be doing this as much for you as I am for myself. You can't be happy with our constant bickering - I must drive you up the wall."

"Yes you do and I must wind you up the wrong way as well."

"You know full well you do, and that is the reason I feel we should call it a day and live apart." After a few seconds of silence she continued.

"But you have surprised me, in fact you have taken me aback. I don't think in all the years we have been married you have ever expressed anything like a feeling. Why does it take a crisis like this to get you to say anything about our relationship?"

"Well, I'm not very good at it, am I?"

"No, you're not."

Joyce had not been filled with enthusiasm for the divorce after her discussions with the solicitor. There was a lot more to think about than she had originally thought, and to her, the last few moments had come as almost a blessed relief, although no way was she going to expose that feeling to Hardy. It wouldn't hurt him to sweat a bit, she thought.

"Look," she continued, "you can get to a point where you can't live together and you can't live apart either, and it maybe that is where we are."

That confused Hardy. She continued:

"If, and it's a big if, we do stay together, we can't change - we may say we will, but I would put money on it that within a couple of weeks we would be back at each other's throats, and the question I have to ask myself. Is that the price I am willing to pay to stay together? Frankly, Hardy, you have to ask yourself the same question."

Hardy knew deep down that that was a first-class analysis of where they were. But Joyce went on:

"What you have just said about you caring for me does make a difference, Hardy. But is it that you actually care about me, or about the situation having to change, having your comforts disrupted, having to make new relationships and put some effort into life - which frankly nowadays you put hardly any effort into life - or is there a genuine wish to stay with me?"

This was all heavy stuff, probably the most heavy stuff they had ever talked about. In fact probably the only stuff they had ever really talked about since the baby problem.

"Mm." If he was honest, really honest, he didn't really know. "It also works the other way round, doesn't it? I mean, there would be lots of disruption to your life and we would both be considerably worse off." Hardy made the point.

"Yes of course, and that's the trade-off. The easy thing to do is to just drift on, but I want more out of a relationship than just constant arguing and bickering and snipes. I mean, what makes me do most of the sniping, what causes it. I am still in a state of confusion, Hardy, and I am still in the process of having to weigh all this up."

"So where are we? Do I get a letter from your solicitor in the morning?"

She hesitated but decided there was no point in not being absolutely honest. This seemed to be the theme at the moment, honesty.

"No. He sent me away to think things over and then if I decide to go ahead I have to contact him again and he would then arrange an arbitration meeting. That's not any form of reconciliation - that is a meeting to decide what we do with everything. So as it stands at the moment the ball is in my court. Or of course, it could be in yours if you decided that this is a good idea."

"Well, I don't think it is. My real thoughts are that we would be completely lost with out each other, and I am asking you to hold on."

"Hold on for what?"

Hardy didn't know. But she did agree to give matters more thought.

And then, Hardy arranged an adventure. A protest. A protest at the lack of counselling services that existed to help divorcing couples and the general way in which society dismissed older people, viewed as no longer relevant or useful.

CHAPTER 6

It would soon be time for something to eat - after all, they had missed their elevenses and none of them would suffer the hardship of missing lunch as well. Was it a good idea to start the venture before lunch, or should they have an early lunch to give them a clear run in the afternoon?

"Didn't you all bring sandwiches as discussed?" asked Hardy, somewhat sharpish.

"I have," proclaimed Bert. Bert had slowly over the morning's activity become a puce colour and beads of sweat were running down his face. Of course he had brought sandwiches: he obeyed the rules, always,

"But after all this running about it would be nice to sit down quietly in the gardens here and eat them now."

"I agree," said Ken.

"Look, we're all a bit stressed and tired I think - perhaps a break with something to eat might get our sugar levels back up and give us a second wind," Olly interjected.

Sarah found a seat next to Bert. She had not had much to do with Bert. She knew he was ill and admired him for putting himself 'up' for today. He was obviously not finding it easy and she suspected that he might be in some sort of pain as his face frequently contorted itself as the body braced against the trauma.

Hardy was strolling around the benches on which his 'army' had perched themselves, informing them that new decisions had been made by the 'executive' and that they were to get the noon ferry, and that all actions were very much 'on'. That gave them a good forty minutes to relax in the glorious warm sunshine and just stare at the harbour. Another large cross-Channel ferry was making her way out towards Caen. Enthusiastic passengers waved and some on the shore waved back, complete strangers joined together by the sense of departure. The ship was called the Mont St Michel and Sarah remembered the time she had sailed on the vessel with her late husband. They had used it quite often when holidaying on the continent of Europe. They would drive, taking their time of course, right the way down from the north coast of France to the Mediterranean coast around Perpignan. They were very pleasant times and she remembered them with fondness. There was nothing more she wished for right now, watching that rather large car ferry going out, than she to be on it with her husband. But, come on Sarah, she thought, you are going to have to make do with the Gosport ferry.

Olly was on his mobile, probably to his wife, who was probably again questioning the whole mission.

"Problems?" asked Hardy, always slightly worried whenever he saw anyone on a mobile.

"No, not at all, just finding out what was for supper tonight, so I could gauge what to eat now."

This sort of decision is not an issue when you are young, but when you get older these little things become vitally important. Olly was, on the advice of his loving wife, about to embark across the road to Greggs and buy a Cornish pasty. That would have vegetable in it as well as meat and would stave off what appeared to be a permanent condition with Olly, that of feeling hungry.

The fact that it had been a mistake to mention his trip to Gregg's suddenly dawned on him.

"Oh if you are going over there …" What a pain, he thought; it reminded him of being back at work when the person who gave in first and needed to make their way across the road to the baker's, was awarded with the 'can you get me?' line.

Sarah

Sarah was well travelled. She had been born on the island of Malta. She had been brought up in quite a Catholic puritanical way: Malta in the 1960s was very Catholic, even to the point that the local bus driver often having an effigy of the Virgin Mary next to his driving position.

Sarah would have joined her family on a Sunday evening, when most of the island seemed to turn out to be 'seen' on the main street in Valetta, not doing anything much but just walking up and down, saying hello to distant semi-strangers and chatting to family and friends. It was habitual and it felt safe.

In the mid-60s sailors would often join those throngs, sailors from the Royal Navy, and then sometimes Yanks from the American Navy. The Americans assumed an air of superiority, perhaps because they were indeed superior, but Malta was loyal to her old friend Great Britain. It wasn't until a few years later when Dom Mintoff, as Prime Minister of an independent Malta made overtures to the Chinese, that attitudes changed a little. She remembered the Chinese well; many had been sent to build a dry dock in the old Naval Base, all dressed in their suits, unable to communicate much because of language but still managing to convey that they were turned on by the very beautiful Maltese girls, of whom Sarah was one. She knew as she got older she would run to fat just as her mother had done, and she decided to make the most of her younger years. In common with most teenagers she had rebelled against the established order, often embarrassing her parents with her dress sense.

They were not poor, in fact quite the opposite as her father was an engineer, first with the Royal Navy as a civilian, and then with one of the Greek shipping companies that were somehow making a fortune at the time. It had been that money that had facilitated them moving to better accommodation, away from the crowded streets of Valetta. Sarah had done well enough at school but had not shone. However, she had done sufficiently well to be offered a place at the University of Exeter in England. Whilst excited by the prospect and supported by her parents, she was also nervous at leaving home. This would be the first time in her life that she would be on her own and in a strange country. She was envied by her Maltese peers, with: "Wow, you're going to London, to Carnaby Street and Wembley." She needed to point out that Exeter was some hours' travel from London and she would probably not be able to afford to travel to London that often.

She had loved Exeter University at first but as winter drew on and dark depressing clouds queued up in the Atlantic to discharge their albeit life-giving rain over the West Country of Britain, she began to long for the warmth and sunshine of Malta.

Home-sickness had set in until, that is, she met Carlos.

Carlos, like her, was dusky skinned with long black hair,

hair which would be frowned on in Malta. But Carlos was Spanish and the pair spoke almost in tongues, part Spanish, part Maltese, part English. Their relationship quickly became an 'event'. Her first love affair. But Carlos was a prat, offset by his brilliance with the guitar. He would play classic Spanish guitar to a group of Spanish and Portuguese friends as well British students and his skills were universally applauded. But with that came this 'artiste' approach to life. He could never cut certain fingernails, regardless of the damage he had sometimes done to Sarah's more delicate parts. "No," he would say, "a true guitarist uses nails as a plectrum - how dare you suggest otherwise!" He was constantly late and would finish performances on such a high that it would take several hours to come down, with the consequence that Sarah was expected to be on the same high when all she really wanted to do was sleep. Inevitably he became too much for her, and she applied herself to her studies that during their relationship had been somewhat neglected and she had consequently fallen behind. Carlos had accepted the situation with little bother, a trait that she would find was not uncommon among her enthusiastic suitors.

Sarah was studying Business and in particular modern methods of accounting and use of the new technologies just beginning to emerge. Exeter was one of the first to instal a new-fangled computer. It was enormous but could calculate complex number issues in seconds. Sarah was in the right business at the right time, with the consequence that after her degree, she applied for a research grant. She got it, and was also sponsored by IBM, who took her into their stable.

IBM eventually sent her to Paris, where she met the man who would become her husband, a man who could keep her in the way to which she could easily become accustomed.

Frederick had been an engineer connected to the oil and gas industry and had been seconded to IBM by his company to examine the future uses of the exciting new technologies that were emerging.

Their marriage had not been a particularly happy one and they increasingly spent more and more time apart. She had gone back to Malta for a long time to live with, and care for, her ageing parents, but the move back there had set up an enormous chasm between her and her husband and between the two children, one of each sex, and their father. Sarah had taken the kids with her to Malta, placing all sorts of tensions on the marriage. Even her parents, while appreciating the dutiful daughter being there for them, occasionally mentioned that perhaps she should pay her husband Frederick some attention, at least inviting him for holidays or other breaks. Sarah was more concerned with her mother and father: she almost dismissed the husband, but the marriage survived, with both parties believing both in the sanctity of the marriage and that it was necessary to work at it.

Sarah could not understand herself. Examined on paper, Fredrick was a good husband. They owned and maintained a small flat in London. The children were being educated in Wellington, not far from her old university. He had accommodated her need to look after her parents, who eventually died within three weeks of each other. She sold their property on Malta and they were set up to buy a more substantial property down in the West of England. It was, she thought, financially looking rosy. But why, and she kept asking herself the same question, why oh why did she really not care whether he was with her or not? The paper exercise would indicate perfection as a partner, so the question perplexed her until the shock of a lifetime came, when he was diagnosed with cancer of the liver. He was devastated and surprisingly, so was she. He did not deserve that.

Sarah's husband had died some six years previously. She had nursed him. She nursed him because she was Catholic and had taken vows to her God that she would take care of him in sickness. She would not renege on those vows. It had been hard. The two children were now fully grown and living their lives, one in Singapore, the other in Cologne in Germany, and had little time, or indeed inclination, to contribute any time or input to their father during his illness. 'Dad' was dying of cancer of the liver, undoubtedly the result of heavy drinking in the many hotel bars inhabited over forty or so years.

They had settled in Gosport to deal with Fredrick's illness. Gosport was level, there was only one manmade hill, so it was popular with those who relied on mobility aids to get around. Frederick got great joy from being taken to the harbour entrance where he could watch, sometimes for hours, the ships that went to and fro, and most of all he loved to see the big car ferries heading for France. Sarah and Fredrick had used Portsmouth in the last few years as a route to the Mediterranean, to visit her relatives who had now moved to Turkey. They always had so much luggage that it was cheaper to drive, and also the journey became part of the break, staying in their favourite hotels. It was in these later years that they were probably the most happy, and most together.

Royal Naval ships were now less and less in evidence, and it was with sadness that Fredrick, as an engineer, watched ship after ship being towed out of the harbour to go to scrap, ironically most going to Turkey to be broken up.

Sarah had battled for him. She had experienced health services in the USA and France and now in the UK. In

France you paid up front, and had to go through French bureaucracy to get your money back, but the service was good. In the USA the medical attention was second to none, and so was the cost. If you were poor in the US, forget it - just suffer. But the UK seemed to fall between the two. She thought of the battles she had fought to get her husband relief from pain, the times she met staff where she had to start telling his story all over again. She was cross. Her husband had paid all the taxes asked of him, yet when it came to pay back it was an uphill struggle.

After his death, she now found herself living alone in town to which she had little connection. She had a sister now living in Turkey, with whom she kept in touch. The children had at the last knockings deemed the death of their father sufficiently important enough to put in an appearance, which lasted for just over a week. Both offspring found it difficult to understand why, out of all the places on the planet that were available to them, their parents had decided on Gosport as a great place to die. To be frank, Sarah had a job to explain it as well, apart from the housing market providing good value for money, and of course when their father was ill, he got great enjoyment by being by the sea, and in particular the sea when being used by ships and boats of all varieties.

Both children had urged their mother to think more long term, looking into a future where she might need someone to look after her, particularly now she was on her own. Sarah had noted, however, that there had been no offer of care from either of the children, not that she would have wanted to go to either Singapore or Cologne, but it would have been nice if they had even offered to plant themselves into some long-term plan. They were still both single and Sarah often wondered whether this inability to sustain a relationship was as a result of their unsettled upbringing. They had departed a couple of days after the funeral, having helped Sarah with paperwork. They had left for their prospective destinations leaving Sarah with little more knowledge of their lives than when they had arrived, and she felt she was left to 'just carry on'.

Although Sarah was reluctant to consider the possibility, she did wonder – because neither child had married – that they might be gay, something that she referred to as 'batting for the other side'. She knew little about gay relationships but from what she read in the *Daily Mail*, gay people seemed too often be promiscuous. She had brought the subject up with her daughter, and it had not been easy.

"Your cousin is having another baby," was Sarah's way of kicking off the subject.

"Is she? How many is that then?"

"Um, that's five, isn't it?"

"Yeah, got to be, and spanning what? Ten years? One every two years - pity her!"

"Why do you pity her? Don't you ever have an urge to settle down and have children?"

"Frankly, mother, no. I just don't seem to have that urge at all - at this moment in time I am free to do as I wish and I like it like that."

"But don't you have, well …" Sarah was finding the whole subject awkward now. "You know, any sort of special person in your life." Sarah was pleased with that; it gave her daughter the ability to answer in any way she felt.

"What you are really asking, mum, is if I am in a relationship with anyone, isn't it?"

"I suppose so." There was a silence.

"Well … are you?"

"No mother I am not. I don't want such complications in

my life at the moment. And before you ask, no I am not gay."

Sarah hesitated but decided to be cool and not react to the last bit, so she eventually said:

"But you know, you can so easily let your life slip away, and at the end you have no one."

"Sorry mum, but you don't have kids just to keep you company in your dotage."

To Sarah, that remark answered more than just her initial question; it put her in no doubt that this daughter had no intention of offering any comfort during her old age, and she had felt so suddenly alone. Her husband dead, her children giving notice of almost abandonment, and miles between her and her sister.

She was tinkering with a decision now to return to Malta - at least there were nieces and nephews there – and at least there was still an ethos of care for senior citizens, which she seemed to have singularly failed to instil in her own children. Added to that, she felt she lived in a town that was pretty parochial, which surprised her as it was a naval town. The inhabitants were friendly enough and would offer to help in times of trouble. Her neighbours had been fantastic during her husband's illness, but like so many towns all over the world, unless you had gone to school in the town, there was an element of being an outsider, being the white of a fried egg and not really penetrating the yoke, so to speak. She had in her travels experienced that same issue many times in her life, but now it seemed more important. She felt she needed to belong. She might well need to return to her island home in the Mediterranean, but at this moment she just didn't feel up to another move.

Sarah tried the Catholic church in search of a sense of belonging, but it had not worked out. It was not as she remembered it from her home in Malta, and so she had drifted to the Church of England, and had met this group of people, and in particular one named Ken.

Ken was also a member of a local political party, the party that is often called the 'Church of England At Prayer'. But he never wore that on his sleeve and it was to be a couple of months before Sarah actually realised that Ken could be the route to another set of people that could become her friends and perhaps fill a void in her life.

Ken and Sarah became good friends, and were, after a few months, generally regarded by the church people as a couple, and by Sarah's children as an item. Sarah, upon announcing over the few 'Skype' moments to her two offspring that she was 'seeing' another man, noticed a marked change by both of them in attitudes. They took an interest, unusually so. What did this Ken do? Was he nice to her? And oh, was he comfortable?

"What do you mean, comfortable?" she had retorted

"So, like, has he got his own house?"

Sarah never swore, but in her head she did, because she had seen through the rather inept question straight away. The grasping little sods were more interested in their inheritance or a threat to it than they were in their mother's happiness.

She reassured her son that Ken and herself only intended to stay really good friends and that he would continue to live in his own house and she in hers. She didn't want to live with another man; she was happy having her own space, as long has she had company to call on and the loyal friendship of others. No, she had told them, she did not want to wash socks and clear up. She did not want that funny familiar smell of urine from a semi-missed pee performed by a male in the middle of the night. She did, however, love his company and she was very fond of him.

"So he is a friend 'with benefits' I suppose mum." Her son had made a statement that also needed an answer.

"What do you mean?"

"Oh come on, mum. Sex, that's what I mean."

Sarah was taken aback by her son's frankness. Indeed in her world it was a little too frank and honest but she did get it: the light shone in on her darkness - it appeared that sex was now a 'benefit'.

"I mean that's good, mum, nothing wrong in it at all -it's good for both of you. Life ain't over yet, is it?"

This was different thinking, particularly in as much it was now her son who was giving her, his mother, a moral steer. "Nothing wrong," he had said. In her day a woman was somebody to be revered and almost fought over. Sex was considered an earned privilege, available only to a very special man and as part of a 'duty' in an effort to procreate and to please her husband. That man was then lined up to give you children and provide for you and the offspring. This new stuff whereby the woman was 'up for it' as much or sometimes more than the male was a world she did not recognise. She accepted that as her marriage had gone on, and life had changed, she had over time started to enjoy sex. She had put this down to the fact that her husband had also got up to date, that he thought of her as much as himself, and that was good. Even though it was not the best marriage in the world, or the happiest, it wasn't the worst, and they had found the level at which things would last out.

"Oh for God's sake" was about the only response she could make. She certainly had no intention of discussing her private life with her son.

"Ken provides me with friendship and also a social circle that I lost when I was looking after your dad. Don't forget I had to look after him by myself, I had little support, so that in turn meant I didn't get out and I didn't meet people. You two never showed your face and if it hadn't been for the kindness and relief of the nurse that came in, I wouldn't have even seen another human being in the day. So the fact that I have a new friend now, I do not either feel guilty or unjustified. Just leave it at that." There: she had said it finally, leaving a rather silent stunned son on the other end of the phone.

With this venture, she could belong, she was part of them, however harebrained the whole thing was, and however successful or unsuccessful it turned out to be, it didn't matter to her – she belonged to a group and was part of a 'couple'.

Ken had reasoned with her that to partake in the activities of various social groups and his own political party was a great idea. It would introduce her to a wider circle of friends and associates, plus her political views found a home with this party. After a couple of weeks of thinking about it, she joined and immediately offered herself as a volunteer to help wherever she could.

A volunteer in such an organisation is quickly put to use. She had not found it easy, however, to be 'included'. Again, all the same old issues came to the fore. It became apparent that these people all knew each other so very well. They went back years and years, and most of them were older than even she was. Like many organisations there was an inner core, and even though you had joined the organisation, this 'inner core' seemed impermeable. Nothing ever said; no one ever said anything other than it was great to have her onboard. Everyone was friendly but somewhere there was just that little gap, just the occasional reminder that she was who she was, a new girl. She had the feeling they had meetings without telling her. The reality was that, of course, they would speak to each other on other occasions - that could not really be called a 'meeting'. Like in many organisations, an issue was often resolved with discussions in the gents' toilets.

She had asked Ken if that were true. He seemed to be several rungs above her on the 'in crowd' stakes, so his comments would tend to be valid.

"Well, I have never really thought about it, but on reflection I suppose there are lots of conversations started in the toilets."

"Good heavens," she had exclaimed.

"Yeah, but I don't think that it's done on purpose, it's probably nervousness."

"Why nervousness?" she enquired, genuinely not understanding.

"Yeah, I mean when you go and stand next to another man who has his gear out already, lots of men find it difficult to 'go', and so to break that up they start talking to the guy next to them at the urinals. And now you come to mention it, you are right. I've actually had expenditure approved back when I was working, at the urinal," Ken added.

Sarah had put aside the thought that had occurred to her that all the big decisions in the world had been made whilst a guy's cock was in his hand. Perhaps, she thought, that's where the expression 'cock up' comes from.

She had volunteered to carry out the duties of a bookkeeper in one of the organisations she had got involved with, quickly got the hang of it, and gained the confidence of those around her. The Treasurer and Chairman just seem to accept whatever she said, and she was pleased by the level of trust they showed in her. In reality, they probably couldn't be bothered to check anything.

Now it wasn't easy adjusting to income derived only from her pensions. Frederick had left her provided for, well enough, but over time her lifestyle and living standard was bound to slowly drop.

It started easily enough. A cash collection had been made at a fund-raising function. She had put in a lot of work on the function, so felt somewhat justified in taking out a fiver towards the money she had spent on drinks - she had earned it after all. That fiver seemed to break a mould; she found that she could take cash out of any collection made because they always gave her the bag containing the money for banking and no one had a clue what was in it. As long as she banked something that looked reasonable, no one ever showed any interest. But this occasional dipping into funds nowhere near gave her security of income; there was more she needed to do. So she had the idea of diverting members' subscriptions through the bank to her account. It wouldn't be noticed and the accounts were seldom audited properly because the organisation was too mean to pay for a proper auditor. This way she was able to add some two hundred pounds a month to her income, enough to buy several good perfumes and the odd bottle of good wine. This 'income' had the added bonus that it was tax-free.

The 'schemes' had now been going on for several months and all seemed fine, except she found sleeping quite difficult and she needed the church more than ever but could not bring herself to visit. She treated herself to expensive handbags again. She had made a rule in her head that she should use the money obtained by these devious methods solely for luxuries so that when it stopped, as indeed she knew she had to at some point, there would be no noticeable change to her ability to live. But she would lie in bed at night, unable to sleep, going over scenario after scenario as to how she might get caught, and other scenarios of how she could end this before she did get caught. She had also become ashamed of herself.

In recent days, before this ferry venture, she had told herself she should 'sort' this transgression out, but one of the problems was that it was giving her a thrill. It was as much about the 'wrongness' of doing this and the adrenalin hike it gave her, as it was about the cash. But she knew it had to stop … one day. If she did get caught, and frankly she could not see how that would happen after her nights of rehearsing the possibilities, it would be a major trauma, not only for her, but her family and probably her relationship with Ken, so she would stop it one day soon.

The problem with the Church of England, she thought, was that it did not offer Confession on the same terms as the Catholic church. You could pray for the 'forgiveness' of sins, but somehow that seemed a bit of a coverall, like an insurance policy that covered everything but actually paid out on very little. So, she argued with herself, the church she attended was not actually providing much help with this little fetish she possessed, for stealing.

Sitting now in the Falkland Gardens, which greets travellers to Gosport from the 'other side', in glorious sunshine and warmth, a gentle breeze wafting in from the Solent, Sarah found herself next to Bert. There was no doubt about it; they were all beginning to feel the stress of the constant delays to the operation and protest. She turned to Bert, asking something she felt was both friendly and neutral.

"Are they, I mean the medical people, looking after you, Bert?" she had asked. Bert looked at her. To be fair, he had never 'studied' her. Sarah obviously dyed her hair - it couldn't possibly be that jet black now, thought Bert. She was dressed very well, matching her skin tone with summer-like colours. He had never really noticed her breasts before: they were huge. He found himself staring at them, watching the rise and fall of the cleavage amply on display from the bright yellow summer frock she wore. Bert realised that he probably was being noticed by her for staring at her breasts and that these days that was totally inappropriate, or so he was told by the BBC. He looked at her sunglasses but could not see her eyes. It gave him no clue as to whether she was cross with him, or had not even noticed his gaze. On the other hand, he quickly thought, she was probably used to it.

"Oh yes, I couldn't be better cared for," he eventually told her, grateful for everything.

She decided not to relay her transactions with the NHS to Bert. A contrast, she thought, to her experience. It had not been good the way they had let her late husband suffer in her eyes. It was over now - there was really no point in alarming others. She had to move on, and that she had done. Frederick's death had left a void. Looking after a sick person tended to take over your life, and when they died, there was a post-death depression, not caused so much by the loss of the loved one, even though that was indeed important, but loss of the project, loss of being needed. She wondered sometimes whether it was like post-natal depression. She was acutely aware that the whole group to some degree was suffering a form of joint depression, the depression brought on by not being really needed by society. But Ken was healing her, healing her slowly from this feeling. If only she could say that about her own behaviour, she thought.

"I hear you lost your husband and that he had this damned condition as well," Bert finally added.

"Yes, it was horrible, and very painful watching the person you love go downhill like that, but I would rather not talk about it if you don't mind." That was wise thing to do, thought Bert, and also a bit of a relief to him.

"No, no, of course not." Bert did not wish to offend or put her into a position she did not want to be in. He had taken his jacket off, his white shirt almost too much in the bright sunshine. The shirt was soaking around the armpit area, confirming Sarah's suspicions that he was finding this a bit too much. His braces held his trousers high and they traveled nearly to his breastbone. A peculiar thought passed Sarah's mind: she thought, however does he get it out of them to go to the loo? And then she instantly rejected the thought as being impure and quite improper to even pass through her mind, and anyway, thinking about it, she realised he would have just slipped the braces off his shoulder.

"Bert, are you sure you want to go on with this? You look to be in some distress to me."

"Oh yes, yes, what else would I be doing?"

"Well resting for one, with your feet up, perhaps in your garden eh?"

"No, it's very nice of you to be concerned, but I must go on. You see I have my reputation to consider - once I give my word, you see, I must adhere to it."

"You are obviously a man of principal, Bert, rare in today's world, but it is patently silly to become ill - you'll put yourself in a position to destroy your health even further if you continue with this venture."

Sarah would home in and just say it. But it always had a ring of truth about it, unlike that nasty Joyce, who would say things just to hurt.

Bert reasoned with himself. He was, it was true, feeling terrible. He was hot and his mouth was dry. He had pains in places new to him, and above all his feet ached. Now he was sitting down, to add to the misery he was feeling tired, and the thought of dragging the damned banners around with him possibly all afternoon was not giving him any comfort at all. He again reasoned with himself that if another person was telling him that he should not go through with it that would be a different matter than jacking out of his own accord. He could also be an actual risk to the operation should he be taken ill.

He thought: this is terrible, he should not be thinking like this, but then it may also be a reflection of what was going on in his body. His brain was telling him that he was not the fit man of a few years back, and that this project was indeed all too much.

Sarah, a woman of perception, spotted that he was weakened. He was, without wanting to be too brutal, a liability to them in this state.

"Let me talk to Hardy, Bert. Let me tell him that it's me, not you, that thinks you should go home and rest."

There was a silence. She reinforced her argument: "You see I think you are a man of honour, and the fact that you are here is honourable, and to be praised, but there comes a time when you need to look after yourself. If you like I will even pop in on the way back home and tell you what has happened. Would you like that?"

He would like that, and she did talk to Hardy.

"He's in a bad way, Hardy, and even with the best will in the world, if he is taken really ill – say on board the ferry – then the whole thing is off, isn't it?"

Again, Sarah had understood the weak spot with Hardy.

Any appeal to him regarding the welfare of Bert would have been less well received, she felt, and she was right. Providing Hardy saw Bert as a liability, then he was prepared to agree to leave of absence.

"Oh well, he better go home then." Hardy had reluctantly relented.

Bert, somewhat dejected but at the same time a little relieve decided to hang the cost, and took a taxi back to his home. It was really hot now, and it was not before time that he got into a taxi.

He struggled to get the banner in the back of the car, and the taxi driver leapt to his help and stuffed it in the boot.

The group stood there, gazing as the taxi took off to take Bert the half a mile or so back to his home.

CHAPTER 7

The departure of Bert had initially sent Hardy into a 'tis was'. He was finding it increasingly difficult to cope with change and Joyce of course wasn't helping with her caustic remarks about his choice of personnel in the first place. Although they were still 'together', or rather living under one roof, their relationship had not improved. They still managed to wind each other up, but neither was actually prepared to break the habit of marriage. They both went through the fantasies of doing so, almost like the 'cold' war, where mutually assured destruction holds both parties to ransom. So, 'being together' continued.

"Look, just shut up will you, unless you've something positive to say – just close it." Hardy was showing signs of stress; he was trying in the politest was to stop her going on.

"Go jump in the harbour - is that positive enough for you?"

"One of these days I swear, I'm going to swing for you."

"Huh, you'll need an army to assist you."

Olly approached. Hardy and Joyce ceased their rather distasteful dialogue, although it was not really necessary because no one took any notice of them anyway. Even though the offers of violence to each other sounded vicious, nothing had ever come of it … yet.

"We'd better get everyone together, hadn't we?" asked Olly.

"Well, those of us that are still doing it, that is," Hardy replied with an edge to his voice.

"What do you mean?" asked Olly.

"Well, Bert's home, sick. I had to put him on sick leave, didn't I?"

"He was homesick? We're only going over to Portsmouth, for pity's sake."

"No, dozy bugger, he has gone home ill - I had no choice but to let him go."

"Well I have to say he wasn't looking good at all, but these are things that we just have to get over, and in true tradition we just carry on, don't we?" Olly was doing what he did best, being positive, but he was also crowding Hardy's space. The stance and body language could be construed as aggressive, but Olly never ever saw it like that. He had leant into Hardy, marginally reducing his overwhelming height, but at the same time he was inches from Hardy's nose. Hardy recoiled, momentarily increasing the distance between noses, and wondering what the issue was.

"What's up with you?" Hardy had picked up on Olly's anxiety, the real reason behind his 'positivity'.

"I can feel an issue coming, I can feel yet another reason for not doing this whole project coming, and that sort of negativity always makes me cross."

"Look, you haven't heard what I've got in mind yet, have you? You're as bad as she is, jumping down my throat before you have even heard anything. Now if you want to be useful, round up the others and let's sit on the wall over there out the way of everyone, and get this show off the ground." It was a rebuke to Olly, and Olly took it, but he had a dark mood come over him - he often did. It was always so sudden, and took little to spark it. Bert going home was not the issue; the issue now was surrounding the leadership of the group and whether Hardy was up to it, to react to a change in plan. And that was what he doubted, and that was what made him cross, and that was in turn followed by the darkness in his head that now engulfed his mood. It was good that Hardy had given him a job; that way he could escape momentarily the likelihood of a major row between them and it would give Hardy time to think of something.

Olly was not unaware of his ability to intimidate. It had been pointed out to him many times back when he was in the workplace, and since, by his wife and one of his very good friends. He had at many meetings caused upsets - people had complained (always afterwards) that he had an overbearing nature and that he was not prepared to listen to other people. It was, he knew deep down, not an unfair criticism.

"See, you've upset Olly as well now," Joyce chimed in.

"You what? What about him upsetting me?" Hardy exclaimed to her. The remark was ignored as usual.

"Well, it doesn't surprise me. I have to put up with your moods and attitudes every bloody day of my life. I just knew this would happen; as soon as anything goes wrong, you can't rise to it, can you?"

Did she actually want an answer to that question, he thought, because if she did he would point one or two things out to her that may very well hurt her big-time. So he ignored it and things petered out as usual and when the depleted group gathered in the corner over by the boatyard, where the public are forced to go inland away from the sea to walk round the yard, Hardy was relatively calm.

His announcement bore the attributes of Churchill. It was slow and deliberate, bordering on a speech.

"I think we all noticed earlier today that Bert was finding things difficult. You know he is suffering with his illness, and the last thing any of us want, I am sure, is to see such a lovely man suffer. It may therefore come as no surprise that I have taken the decision to relieve him of his duties today, and to accept the fact that the man is sick. He has accordingly gone home."

There was a measured 'oh' from one or two.

"He wanted to continue," added Sarah.

"This was not a matter of defenestration - I insisted he go home. I shall keep him informed and shall call in to see him on the way home to make sure he has food and drink."

Mm, thought Ken, that's Bert sorted then for the next ten years. Sarah had a habit of shopping for the British Army, a mothering instinct Ken had put it down to.

"What?"

"What what?"

"That word you used, what the hell is that?"

"Oh right, it means chucking out, comes from chucking out the window, comes from the German word 'fenster' meaning window," Sarah explained.

"Thank you, Sarah, for looking after him and for the lecture. Every day is a school day. However, the assault will need to be rethought through. Ken, will you take the banner? You will need to get up to the top deck as soon as you are onboard, and I suggest now because the lack of manpower, you start fixing it as soon as possible."

Ken was reluctant. Whilst he spoke of action, he himself was now a bit past it, and he had to bend to tie the banners to the side of the railings. Bending was a problem to him nowadays. But he was not given the time to mention his concerns.

"We'll get the next ferry."

"I shall need to get another pensioner ticket," mentioned Kenneth.

"Oh for God's sake, you've had all lunchtime to do that."

"Oh, was that rest period, lunch, then?"

"Of course it was." Hardy was irritated yet again.

"Look sorry, you never made that clear. I thought it was just a break."

"Just go and get your ticket, and hurry up."

Hurry was not a word that came easily to Kenneth. He was also concerned about his mate Ken and his new status as chief banner holder. Did he not need help with the banner? Which indecently raised a question for Ken.

He very quietly asked as to the whereabouts of the banner.

There were blank looks on some faces.

Hardy shouted to Kenneth, who was heading for his new tickets. Hardy shouted again: "Kenneth!" Kenneth did not hear. "Kenneth!"

"Well it must be over there, on that seat we were sitting on." Sarah got up as if to go and search, but it was obvious it was not there, even from where they were standing.

"Hang on a minute, I remember now - Bert getting in the taxi. He had it with him," recollected Sarah.

"Oh" was the exclamation from nearly all involved. It was that sort of 'Oh' that trailed off in key tone. Hardy was more forthright. "Oh bloody hell, are you sure?"

"Thinking more about it, yes I am. The banner got caught between the doors and he practically fell into the taxi. The driver got out and put it in the boot."

"Shit," Hardy exclaimed.

"Mm yes, it's a vital part of our campaign. This is no good. We will be wasting our time if we don't get our message over on the side."

"Stupid old sod," interjected Joyce.

"Now stop that, he wasn't feeling well at all, he wasn't thinking straight, was he?"

Joyce ignored Sarah, as she usually did when someone stood up to her.

"We're going to have to go and get it - we can't go across the water without it. It would be absolutely pointless." Hardy had made a decision, but the question arose as to who would volunteer to go and get the banner from Bert's house?

The day was getting even warmer but a breeze from the sea offered calming relief every three or four minutes. There were, of course, no volunteers. It was going to be a pain: even though it was only about a couple of hundred yards walk to the bus, the thought of the bus, the walk, the talk, (because Bert would not let you off lightly, there was bound to be a frantic search for some conversation) and then the bus back again, with the banner, in this heat, this was not for anyone.

Kenneth, who was by now in the queue buying his ticket, seemed like a good candidate to volunteer. Kenneth could see arms flying around from his place in the queue, and put two and two together. He was best off staying in the queue and then off to the gents'.

Hardy was showing his leadership again. He would do it. Joyce was furious, this time not with Hardy, but with the others. How dare they submit her husband to such a treacherous mission. He was not well himself – could they not see that? But Hardy was gone in a flash and it didn't go unnoticed that he had gone alone.

Ken

Ken was a widower now. His wife had died about eighteen months ago, but he was well cared for by two daughters who took it in turns to check on him at regular intervals. He was now overweight, but had not always been like that, having been an 'all in' wrestler back in the 60s. He had done his 'time' in the RAF, which made him rather a foreigner in Gosport where every other person was either serving in the Navy, or ex Navy. But he still fitted in comfortably, being ex-Services. He had been welcomed to the town of his choice when he had moved there some fifteen years ago after he had retired from his somewhat mundane job as a Housing Officer with the London Borough of Barnet. The guys he had met in Gosport had given him the usual hard time with the age-old RAF jokes. If he heard the old one about the hornets again, he would scream, but it still brought a laugh to those who had not heard it, mainly those under the age of twenty-five.

"Royal Marines are camped in a field when they notice the tent is infested with hornets, so the catch them and eat them. In the same field the Army are camped - they catch the hornets, cook them and eat them. The RAF people notice the hornets … they move to an hotel."

He had become interested in wrestling whilst in the RAF, which provided him with the facilities to train and toughen up. He started going to bouts on weekend leave, when he would travel the booths that ran in funfairs in those days. These booths would invariably have six or seven old boxers and wrestlers who would challenge members of the public. They were always very popular and rowdy crowds and would pay a shilling to go inside and shout at the participants. For local guys from the public, it was their chance to demonstrate to the townspeople that they were not to be messed with. Seldom did it work out like that, however.

Ken's two years of National Service passed with only a short spell abroad in Germany, and upon his demob, he decided to chance his arm fulltime in the wrestling game. The sport, if you could call it that, was very popular on ITV when Saturday afternoon exposure with a commentator called Kent Walton drew large viewing figures. He managed to get two or three appearances on that show, with well-worked routines with the likes of Jackie Pallo and Spencer Churchill, with whom he became great mates. Spencer was also a well-known body builder at the time. Ken and Spencer decided between them on a change of direction and in turn travelled to the island of Montserat in the West Indies, where they bummed around doing DJ work for the local radio station, Radio Antilas. He had got bored after several months and wanted to return to the UK, but alas, had no money, and like so many others of his generation managed to hitch a lift on board a Royal Naval destroyer which took him to Bermuda.

It was there, at the offices of the Naval attache, that he met a young WREN. She had been assigned the job of filling in the numerous bits of paper associated with the rescue of many fun-seeking beggars. His story had intrigued her; it was different to the normal run-of-the-mill gap year student, normally unwashed and slovenly. He had a story to tell and she found him interesting. Most women found him desirable, well muscled and agile, and he now had a suntan to go with the body. Evie found him stimulating and a joy to be with, and that made a world of difference when it came to forming a meaningful relationship. She snared him, and she got him. They were married on her return to the UK, with both sets of parents smiling but somewhat dubious as to the long-term ability of the marriage to survive given Ken's history of being the man-about-town. But survive it did, with Ken changing into quite a caring and responsible person. The marriage more than survived; it matured into a warm loving relationship, with both parties happy in their role and with each other.

The couple produced two daughters, who like so many daughters idolised their dad, and that persisted to this very day. The eldest, Freya, now in her late thirties was a psychiatrist, and worked locally for the health trust in mental health. Ken sometimes thought that with some regret she brought her profession home with her. She would sit down and have heart-to-heart with him, which in his view developed more into a professional relationship than one of father and daughter. It slightly annoyed him when she started to analyse his feelings.

She wanted constantly to talk about her mother's death. Of course he was bloody upset when she died. Wasn't that a normal reaction? But Freya would sit there, leaning forward with a caring expression on her face, demonstrated by a furrowed brow, gazing at him in that manner that only professionals seem to be able to do. He had loved his wife, she had been a mate, and here was his daughter concerned that he was still mourning her.

Freya had been concerned as well with his recurring dreams. She pointed out that recurring dreams are often associated with unresolved issues in a person's life. Had there been unresolved issues with mum, Freya had asked?

"No, none I can think of."

Evie's death had been sudden. She had suffered an

enormous heart attack and had died almost instantly. Here one minute, gone the next.

"Dying so suddenly like that, Dad, often leads to unresolved issues – there's nothing wrong in that." Freya was almost pleading for some enormous confession, but it was not forthcoming.

Ken's recurring dream was bizarre to say the least, and had been going on for over a year now at intermittent intervals. In this dream, he was either on the front at Gosport, or actually on the ferry, when quite suddenly the largest submarine you have ever seen surfaced in the harbour entrance. It was a bizarre submarine, because it had on it two conventional gun turrets, presenting four huge guns, which were disproportionate to even this large submarine. Seawater was pouring from it, and it eventually righted itself from its surfacing, then proceeded up-harbour at about thirty knots, a ridiculous speed for such a vessel and particularly in harbour. The ferry was tossed into the air by the wake from the submarine, as was everything else, but in the dream people just accepted it, and talked about it like it was a secret weapon that the government had just commissioned. The submarine, apparently, was an embodiment of power yet totally useless.

Now he did seek some understanding of this dream from his very intelligent daughter. What bit of unfinished business did this represent, he wondered? Freya viewed it a different way; she thought it might relate to some underlying worry that had yet to manifest itself, and when it did it would literally rock his life. The real issue was the wave, rather than the submarine, she would say. The wave could be cleansing him from previous actions or his worries.

"Oh," he had said. There was not a lot else he could say. He reiterated that he had little idea of any underlying worries, of secrets kept that could surface later to give him concern. In fact he had led quite a boring life since his marriage, apart from the initial few years. Perhaps it went back to the time of - shall we say - misdemeanours. When they married, it was decided he should get a proper job. Wrestling always carried a 'sell by' date, and this date was now beginning to become prominent on his forehead. He could not keep up the physical requirements of the 'show' for any length of time without risk of injury, and as he got older, he might suffer ridicule. Ken was not stupid; he realised that he was now a product on the 'reduced for quick sale' stall. With a family to support he had to find something that was going to provide a regular income. But, of course, he had no skills to offer potential employers and he would have to start at the bottom of the pile in just about any career he chose.

When they had married, Evie had been able to earn straight away, being an ex-WREN Writer; she suited secretarial or PA work easily. She got a job as PA to the director of the Gosport Ferry. At the time Ken had never heard of it, but it offered a job and a position on a pleasant and busy part of the south coast.

They moved to Gosport, renting privately, but he resented the fact that he was not the breadwinner. He set himself up as an 'odd job' man, moving furniture and fixing taps and light bulbs for mainly vulnerable elderly women who could not manage such things. His physique naturally attracted some of these ladies and he found himself being called back for some very odd reasons. It wasn't long before he was providing some ladies with what we might call additional services. He never mentioned the additional 'services' to Evie and she never did find out. He regretted these stupid liaisons - they meant nothing other than cash, but should his wife, Evie, ever find out, he believed it would have been catastrophic for the relationship. But these elderly ladies paid him a lot of money for changing the fuse in a plug. The business surprisingly took off, and whilst most of it was mundane, it put food on the table and savings in the bank that allowed them to have the children.

The dream continued to haunt him. He still mused the issues over.

By now, the women that had needed 'seeing to' were all long gone, so he could discount that as being any threat to any other relationship. While in theory disclosure of such behaviour would now have had no serious effect on his life, it was better, he thought, that his daughters never found out. His stupid actions were from a long time ago now; he had long since dismissed them from his mind. So what other fears might he have? For this he racked his mind. And now here he was queuing up to get onto the very ferry that was to be tossed and washed away by the wake of the submarine.

This turned out to be a 'Road to Damascas' moment. Was his dream a premonition? He found himself ridiculously scanning the harbour, looking for any sign that might mean there was a submarine about to come through the harbour entrance. Quite bizarre, because it had been years since submarines came into Portsmouth Harbour. The last submarine left HMS DOLPHIN, a naval base on the Gosport side of the harbour in 1994, but prior to then, the base could be harbouring as many as twenty submarines, all conventional and in comparison to Ken's dream, very small. Nuclear boats were never based in such a built-up area as Portsmouth Harbour.

His girls were hugely supportive of his new relationship with Sarah. In fact she was a blessing because she relieved them of certain things and Sarah also provided their dad with company.

His daughters had been delighted when he announced to them one day that he had met a lady called Sarah. She had gone to the Spanish group at the local library and he had now introduced her to the church.

Freya was particularly delighted at the modern and refreshing way that her dad and Sarah were approaching things. Nothing too complicated, Ken had told her, just friends, or something a bit more?

His political activity also gave him an outlet, letting him sound off when he wanted and providing him always with something to do should he run out of 'normal' stuff. Today, Ken intended to speak to the press himself. He had been selected to run for council in the next elections which would be in the following May. Today would be an ideal time to get noticed, and for a great cause: the welfare of older people. He intended to support the group on their calls to include the Gosport Ferry into the bus pass scheme.

Of course, he realised that this was very unlikely to happen given the financial constraints on the local authorities, but things like that in politics do not matter. He could say whatever he pretty much wanted in order to get elected, knowing full well the public would swallow it if it were a popular cause. So he saw his motive for this scheme as perfectly legitimate.

There was one problem with his plan. Joyce. She, and at the very least Hardy, were the nominated people to speak to the press. Would Ken get a look in?

"Where's our beloved leader?" Kenneth asked, returning from the gents'.

"Gone up to Bert's to retrieve the banner."

"Yes, I notice no one else offered, leaving my Hardy to do yet another job." Joyce was standing up for her husband. This was all very confusing for those that had not studied the peculiarities of the human psyche. One minute he was the worst human being on the planet, the next, nearly a hero.

"I'd have gone if I'd have known, but I was over there getting a ticket." Kenneth lied, everyone knew he lied, but no one challenged him.

"Well, all we can do again is sit and wait," said Olly.

There were benches all along the seafront that faced the busy Portsmouth Harbour. Most of them reflected a memoriam for some dear departed citizen of Gosport. It was to these benches that the remaining 'crew' turned to.

Olly sat with Kenneth, the Kenneth who has just got his ticket. To be frank he would sit with anyone other than Joyce. The other Ken found himself on a bench, with perfect views of the harbour, with a young woman and her baby. Joyce went to the ladies' with Sarah.

Hardy was hot. Very hot by the time he got to Bert's. He approached the house; he had never been there before, which on reflection seemed odd. He regarded Bert as a friend, but the sort of friend you see on Sunday at church, and at the occasional church 'do'.

The front door was brown and had probably been that colour since the house was built around one hundred years ago. It had a bell which worked on a spring, wound up from the inside by merely twisting the bell over its housing. It worked: a sharp sound of a bell with loads of pent-up energy. So different to the 'wireless' model that Joyce had insisted they invest in, with little batteries, both outside the house and inside on the actual unit. Hardy always felt that there was only a fifty percent chance of the thing working.

Bert still wore a tie, but had at least removed his jacket. The problem with that was that it was exposing huge damp patches around his armpits, a sight that Hardy did not find particularly attractive. Bert seemed surprised to see Hardy at the door. It had not dawned on him that he had inadvertently taken the banner away with him.

"Hardy, have you come to get me back?"

"No, no, you are far from well enough to continue, particularly in this heat."

"So what do you want then?"

"The banner, you twerp!"

There was a blank look on Bert's face.

"The banner?" he repeated to Hardy.

"Yes, Bert, the banner, that thing you have been carting round with you all day - you took it with you in the taxi."

There was a few moments of silence. Bert was now visibly confused.

"But I am sure I haven't got it, Hardy."

"What! You took it," exclaimed Hardy, now losing a little of his patience.

"It's not here, I'm sure. But let me check. I mean I haven't been upstairs since I got back so if I did have it, it would be down here."

"If you haven't got it, where is it then?"

"Oh look Hardy, this is very rude of me - please come in and we can check the ground floor together, because I haven't been upstairs."

Hardy was less keen to do that; he did not want this visit to be expanded into a social call and by going in, that would easily be achieved. On the other hand he did not want to offend Bert, so reluctantly he passed the threshold. It was a long passageway which snaked past the stairs, and on to the kitchen. There was a faint smell of gas, which Hardy guessed was coming from an ancient cooker. It was a huge kitchen, with a stout wooden table at the entry end, surrounded by chairs where the leather of the pads had long since worn through. There was a carpet at the entrance end, which went to flagstone tiles at the other end, which also had a door that led out to the garden through a sort of outhouse. It immediately struck Hardy that the place was miles too big for one man. Poor Bert was rattling around in the place like a dried pea in an empty metal bucket.

"Now, Hardy, this is the only room I have been in," announced Bert in a concerned manner.

Indeed, Bert's jacket was slung over a chair, and on the table was a bottle of Three Barrels brandy. Bert had obviously gone straight to it and, thought Hardy, who could blame him?

"So you see, it's not in here, is it?"

Hardy looked around. There were lots of other things but nothing resembling a banner.

"Here, let me pour you a brandy. I have had one - thought it may help me nod off."

"Oh God, no," protested Hardy.

"Go on, it'll keep you going through all that you have to go through this afternoon, and we can sit and think what could have happened to the banner."

The offer was too good. Hardy was not known for turning down the odd tipple. Indeed, it was one of the constant battles that Joyce had with him, using many schemes to reduce his alcohol intake, which she had deemed as excessive. The kitchen was dark and cool, and perhaps Bert was right: a brandy might indeed benefit him. But Hardy was still cautious; he was aware of the devil within him.

Bert poured Hardy what seemed like a bucket full. Hardy had no intention of drinking all of it, that was until he did. The banner must still be in the taxi, that was the only place it could be - they came to a joint conclusion.

Hardy's mobile came out to ring his wife. The taxi would have gone back to the taxi rank next to the Falkland Gardens. He was not good with a mobile phone. He found them cumbersome with his sausage-like fingers, but as Joyce was plumbed in to his contacts it was easy to ring her. This was what mobiles are for, he told Bert, who looked marginally impressed. "Bert thinks the banner is still in the taxi. It's certainly not here - can you check it out, babe? It was a Ford Focus, a grey one."

Joyce, somewhat bemused to be called 'babe' after all these years and a little concerned that such language was out of character, did however decide to comply and not query the remark.

Yes, the taxi driver did have it; he had put it in the boot and was going to return it to Bert next time he was up that way. Hardy could relax, but should get back down to the ferry now as quickly as possible.

Hardy had had time for another brandy while Joyce had found the taxi, and the whole project didn't seem quite as important after that second bucket full. On the contrary. When Bert had told him that his prognosis was not good, and at best they reckoned he had two months, life suddenly took on a different perspective for Hardy.

"Every day is important Hardy. Why oh why does it take cancer to make you realise that? Is it just that you now have an end date? But then we've had an end date ever since we have been born, haven't we?"

"Bloody 'ell, Bert, I'm sorry, I didn't realise it was as bad as that. Bloody 'ell."

"It's OK Hardy, few people do. You know, I always thought I would go to pieces, thought I would make a real song and dance of it, but I don't think I have, have I?"

"No, you certainly haven't."

"Just goes to show doesn't it? You don't know what strength you've got until it's tested."

"I think you are very brave," Hardy announced, rather more slurred than normal.

"Nonsense, you hear this all the time on the telly, people saying how brave some one is who has a terminal illness, but it's not brave at all - you've no bloody choice, have you Hardy? I think bravery is when someone knows the possible outcomes of a situation and is presented with choice, and for the welfare of others continues to make that choice."

This was profound stuff for Hardy. There was a tear running down his cheek; he put his arm around Bert.

"Bert, it's time we looked after you. You will not go without, I'm telling you, we'll guide you to the sunset. Bert, can I use your loo?" Bert felt a lot better knowing he was to be 'guided' to the sunset!

Hardy was feeling really good. Sod the others and Joyce, they could wait: it was important to stay with Bert for a bit. This was what the church taught, and this was his duty. It wasn't the drink talking, he told himself, careful not to miss the awaiting toilet pan. But at that stage, it never was the drink talking. He looked around.

The toilet was not healthy. Even though most of the stain was limescale it still put Hardy off a bit. This was the sort of issue Bert needed help with. Bert was not able to bend too well and things like this needed doing, stupid things like the light bulb not working, so Hardy had to leave the door open to see, there being only one very small window in the single downstairs toilet.

"Do you have a bulb?" Hardy asked on return. Bert didn't. Hardy would get him one – this was a mission now, a small but practical one which Hardy could cope with. He would pop into a supermarket on the way back, and call into Bert to let him know how things had gone, and replace the bulb.

"I am very disappointed in today, Hardy. This thing really meant something to me, at last a chance to make a difference, albeit simplistic. For once I was shouting, and having got to that position, my health has let me down. Do you know, Hardy, this is the first time I can think of in my life whereby my body has dictated what I do, rather than the other way round, and it hurts, it really hurts." Bert was upset; the brandy was having a melancholy effect on both of them.

Hardy had one for the road before he left. As he opened the front door into the glorious sunlight, he felt really good. He felt almost light on his feet and around him everything seemed to have clear definition, things were going to turn out OK, and he could do his good turn for Bert, with little disruption to his own life.

"There he is." Joyce had spotted him. His gait had changed, she thought, and not for the better.

"He's had a stroke I tell you," she shrieked, "He's had a stroke."

The others looked round. He certainly didn't look as good as when he left, but he didn't look good then either. There was a change, and Olly launched himself over towards the approaching Hardy.

"Are you OK, Hardy?"

His reply was not exactly slurred, but not crystal clear either. But as soon as he opened his mouth, Olly could smell the alcohol on the breath.

"You had a drink, mate."

"Just a couple. Bert's in a bad way – he needed my company for a lille well, um, while."

Joyce needed to be got off the phone to the emergency services, and pretty quickly.

"He's what?" She seemed to need confirmation.

"To put it bluntly Joyce, he's pissed."

She made her apologies to the nice lady dealing with her dramatised 999 call, explaining briefly that the diagnosis of her friend had been incorrect, and apologising for wasting their valuable time.

"My God!" Joyce exclaimed. She was lost for words, which presented itself as a silence. A silence for enough seconds for the others to get out of range.

Ken was still talking to the woman with the baby, and that seemed a natural gathering point to which they headed, leaving Hardy and Joyce to sort each other out.

"You take the biscuit, don't you?" Joyce gave no room to answer. "You disgust me. You are letting all these people down. How bloody dare you, drinking on such an important day."

The 'babe' bit suddenly made sense to her - the bastard had been on his way to this state when he spoke to her.

"Where did you get the drink?"

"Listen, Bert gave it to me, he's dying, he's finished. I needed to be with him, and he needed me to be with him for a bit."

She was actually taken aback by that.

"You haven't just left him have you? Did you call an ambulance or something?"

"Oh, no, he'll be alright this afternoon, it's in a month or so he'll die. So you see, I thought being with him for just a few moments was more important … get it?"

"No excuse for the state you are in; you didn't need to get pissed up like this."

The bitch was right of course, she always bloody was, even on a matter of life and death. The thing was that his body seemed to be able to process alcohol quite quickly, and the effects of it were already beginning to wear off. It was no longer pleasant and he started to feel the need to 'top up', so to speak.

Joyce, on the other hand, was crowing that she had done her bit for the day - she had retrieved the banner - and also felt the need to remind Hardy that if he had phoned Bert in the first place the journey would have been unnecessary, and they could have avoided a further delay.

Hardy somehow knew that even if peace broke out now between them, this incident was stored for later, and to be repeated more times than the BBC had repeated 'Homes under the Hammer'.

CHAPTER 8

Ken seemed to be enjoying himself chatting to the young lady on the bench. Perhaps it was his age, but he seemed to find it easy to talk to young ladies. They never put up barriers now, unlike when he was younger and muscled up. Ken realised that he was old enough to be her grandfather, and perhaps that's how she viewed him. He had no need to 'chat her up', so his conversation was unconsciously non-threatening to her, and she responded accordingly.

Sarah found it amusing, and to some degree reassuring. She left him to it and had sat with Joyce.

The girl had asked Ken 'what's happening?' which alarmed him a little. Was she on to them? But then realised that this was a perfectly innocent question, often used by younger people. He was semi-honest with her, telling her the truth that they were a group of older persons, lobbying for better things for older people. Her eyes had lit up. It transpired that she too was almost a revolutionary when it came to the care of elderly people.

"I worked in a care home. We mainly looked after older people that for whatever reason couldn't cope in their own home," she told him, now leaning in towards him. She believed, she said, that most homes were an insult to the human being, and that elderly people were often judged on what they had become, rather than what they had been.

"It almost seems the moment you stop paying National Insurance, you become forgotten. The state fails you all, or that's the way it seems. I mean the whole system of care in this country needs overhauling. We do well in keeping people alive, but not so well in keeping them comfortable and happy."

Ken was delighted to hear such an enlightened view from such a young person. At first glance, this young lady would have come over as a bit of a slut, dressed as she was in hardly anything, but the constant lesson Ken had learned in his life was 'don't judge a book by its cover.' Her little one was fast asleep in what Ken would have called a pushchair, yet she constantly referred to as a pram. It was almost like a magic trick when she produced from the 'pram' some pieces of paper.

"Read this, if you would," she implored. "I have written it down like … well, like a story. The thing is, mate, it's true, it's the story of a thing me brother … he's a lot older than me … did, and its the sort of thing I really believe in. The lady in the story spoke to me at the end for a real long time, she was so cool, and the whole thing did me head in. I want to try and get this published … see what you think, will you?"

Ken took the papers, totally unaware of what was happening with the others, and indeed by this point he was not really concerned. This young lady was really worth talking too and seemed so genuine. He started to read.

"Can I just leave Jamie with you while I nip over to the loo? If he wakes, I doubt whether he will, just give him a bottle which is in the basket. I promise I won't be long - need to change, if you know what I mean."

Ken did know what she meant, although it had been many years since he had heard that. Even so he was somewhat surprised that she had volunteered such information to a relative stranger. It was probably an indication as to how far removed he was from that generation; the girls and women he had met in his life never disclosed such information until their relationship had been somewhat more intimate. At first he was reluctant to assume the responsibility for a baby, but the toilets were only a few yards away behind them, so he saw little problem. He would read her story while she was gone. It read:

"You are joking, aren't you?"

"No, I couldn't be more serious. I want to move the care of the elderly on, and into the twenty-first century. We still deal with the old in the same way as they did in the 50s. Society has moved on, and the care industry should reflect it."

"Sorry, but I still think you will find it difficult to get a son or daughter to put their parent in your home with that sort of policy, let alone social services."

"I think I will, I think society is ready to reject the traditional home where elderly people are just put in a chair and gaze into the middle of the room. People want more now, and I am going to have a try."

The adverts went out in the local press and relevant magazines.

"A home for the elderly that cares about the needs for a generation that back in the 60s stretched social boundaries. Here they can continue to stretch all sorts of boundaries."

Initially, Robert was inundated with telephone enquiries, to the surprise of his sceptical wife. She was much more pragmatic, and understood that a business founded on a conviction was not necessarily the ideal model for success. Her Scots temper had shown itself of late, and it was beginning to affect their relationship. However, there followed several visits, and within seven weeks four residents were in situ. They were all financing themselves, all well educated, but not quite firing on all cylinders now. This was key to Robert; he felt if he could get to these people before degeneration of the brain set in, he could keep the spark of life going at a better level than conventional ways of care. Robert was trying to balance his occupancy rate equally between men and women, but that was proving difficult and failing to attract women was becoming a major concern. He noticed that most female prospects seemed to fall off at the interview stage.

"It's a lovely home, Rob, very clean, modern and well staffed. What you reckon, mum?" Sue's question was more of a statement, mum felt. Mum had noticed the preamble. Sue seemed to be treating this like choosing a new pair of shoes, rather than a life-changing decision.

Mum was confused. Did she really have to come here?

She had lived on her own since her husband died some twelve years ago, and had grown quite used to her own company and routines. She had fallen about six weeks ago, breaking a collarbone, and she had been lucky not to have had more damage. That had been the final straw for daughter Sue. Her two brothers didn't like the idea of 'mum' going into any sort of home - it was a subject they were putting off doing anything about. But as Sue had pointed out to them, it wasn't them who went round every day, or even every week, was it? They took no responsibility for her, and it was, she thought, so unfair of them to cast doubt on her motives. Sue knew what it was about; it was the business of selling the house, and that total hopelessness of seeing their inheritance being spent day by day on their mother's own care and accommodation. Well, tough, thought Sue, Mum will be well cared for here, and unlike her brothers, she believed that was the main thing for her.

"Thank you, Sue," said Robert. "This is a progressive home, challenging the norms of care homes. We believe in as much freedom as we can safely give our residents."

"Did you hear that mum? It's progressive here. You'd like that wouldn't you, because you've been a Liberal thingy all your life haven't you?"

Mum stared back at her. Stupid cow, mum thought, hasn't got a bloody clue what I've been.

"I get my own room, don't I?" asked Mum. She needed reassurance: the word 'progressive' meant so many things these days.

"Of course you do, but we do encourage you to mix as much as possible with the others. So we have a lounge as well as a dining room where you can socialise, and sometimes there is entertainment, as well as a TV. We think it is a good idea to watch a good drama or documentary together, and then hold a general discussion with views expressed about the issues raised."

"There you go, mum, you are always shouting at the telly, now there will be someone to listen to you." Sue felt more and more satisfied with the ethos of this home. She was becoming convinced that Mum would eventually be very happy here.

Mum needed to think, she needed time; this was all so sudden and there were lots of things to sort out, like whether she would have to sell her home and how long it would take. It all seemed a bit final, no going back.

Mum could not believe the charges, and she also couldn't believe what her house was worth. She could see the maths, *forty-eight thousand a year to live in the home would give her ten years, she worked out. If she lasted that long, she reasoned she probably wouldn't care by then anyway.*

The kids would have nothing, she thought, and her natural instinct was to give them a better start in life than she had had. Then it occurred to her that they already had their own houses, they were in their mid-forties and they went abroad on holiday every year; they had cars and ate at restaurants just about every weekend. She had never had the luxury of such disposable income at that age. She and her husband had saved, had four jobs between them and had only one holiday in the first ten years of their marriage. Perhaps she should not worry too much about them; perhaps this home which was clean, modern and progressive should be the home of her future.

Her room was bright, and full of sunlight when she occupied it on that late April morning. It was warm and welcoming. There was a smell of polish, and her private bathroom gave off an aroma of roses, which matched the pastel shades of pink on the walls and carpets. Mum's initial feelings were of being OK. For Sue, different emotions prevailed.

Sue had come with her, fussing and crying at just about every juncture. Sue had felt more and more terrible about 'dumping' mum in this home, or any home come to that. Somehow these pathetic boxes containing her mum's mementos filled her with a sense of finality. She questioned herself. Was it just for her own convenience, was it just that she was fed up going round every day, even frightened as to what she might find? She was now filled with guilt, and of course Mum was not helping to eradicate that feeling. In fact in an awful sort of way she was actually enjoying Susan's discomfort, and was making the most of the situation, saying that she thought her sister Beryl would be pleased, and that her neighbours had all said they would pop over every so often. "So I'll be alright, Susan, there is no need to worry."

Mum's first meal in the home was lunch.

It was quite different to other homes - all residents sat round a large table. In the centre was a serving wheel, whereby you could reach for the contents of a carafe of red or white wine.

She was joined at the table by four male 'friends'. That's what they were going to be, she had been told: 'friends'. She had been brought to the table. The staff, she was told, were making their own minds up as to her mobility and vulnerability. Could she help herself? Yes she could, and if she wanted to help clear up the dinner things, that too would be OK. The table could easily accommodate ten, so with just five there, there seemed plenty of room for this huge man who now appeared. He sat, with acres of flesh hanging over the chair. He sat in the chair next to her, and she felt like he was invading her space, and it made her slightly uncomfortable. He smelt of a cheap aftershave.

"New?" he asked.

"Yes." She had no further conversation to encourage, but it didn't put him off.

"Well none of us have been here long, it's a fairly new home."

"So I understand," she replied.

"I must say it's great to see a woman here at long last."

"Yeah, we've been a good two weeks without one."
Another voice cropped up.

Mum was now getting uncomfortable. It had been years since she had been in an environment like this, where she found men threatening. If this goes on, she thought, she would not be staying here. She needed to feel comfortable wherever she lived - that surely was a human right, even at her age.

A member of staff entered. It was a woman, thank God for that, at least one more female to talk to, Mum thought.

"Hi all." She was hyper cheery, too much so, and she spoke in a slight Scottish accent. She had red hair to match the accent.

"I want to introduce you guys to Barbara, who has now joined us. Barbara, let me introduce you to Maddison, Ron, Brian and Pinky."

Pinky, she thought, what a funny name, and wasn't Maddison a girl's name anyhow? Each one had nodded as the red-headed staff member had gone round the table.

The Scots lady deposited her rather large frame on an empty chair: she was not done yet. She had lots more to say about the 'home' and its progressive approach. "We want this to be more of a holiday camp than a rest home. Why would you want to rest, one has to ask? Barbara, the bar is open from twelve daily. It's not always manned because we trust you to put in the book what you have consumed. Obviously if you are on any medication that prohibits the consumption of alcohol we would ask you to refrain, but here's the difference in this home: it's your call. Got it? These guys get it, don't you?"

"Mm yes," said Pinky "But what about old Jock who died last week? Only been here three days, consumed a bottle of scotch, and was dead in the morning."

"His call," she said.

"It wasn't just the Scotch. Jock had taken one of those Viagra things that you put behind the bar as well. Said he was going to get on the internet thingy and find himself a woman for the night."

"His call," she insisted. "So basically, Barbara, you can do what you want here, and to quote the old Mamas and Papas song, do what you wanna do with who you want to, yeah?"

Jock had sometimes joked that they put Viagra in the tea - it had had no effect on the residents but stopped the biscuits going soft when dunked.

"I like to try and keep fit, so can I go swimming once or twice a week?" asked Mum.

"It's the best exercise you can get and yes of course. Do you drive? Because we have a car you can borrow to get there if you want."

Barbara was amazed. No, she had given up her licence after her last fit: the man at the ministry said it was too dangerous for her to drive so she relied on public transport now.

"I can take you, I'd like to do that." A new voice, Ron.

"Ron's an excellent driver, we've all been out with him several times haven't we, Ron?"

Ron didn't answer: it sounded patronising but it was probably not meant to be.

Barbara looked at Ron. He had a kindly face, jovial and warm. He gave her what seemed to be a genuine smile, which put her for the first time somewhat at ease.

"Now, Barbara," the red-haired Scot started again in earnest. "We have been through your questionnaire and the information your daughter gave us, and we have assessed you as being in little need of attention. Of course we will check on you both morning and night, just to make sure."

"Didn't check on Jock, did you." More of a statement than a question.

"You know full well we did. He was in bed when Mr Murray checked, and in the survival position, so let's not have any of that talk. Anyway, I doubt whether Barbara is in the habit of consuming a bottle of Scotch per night, are you?"

"No, of course not. One G and T and I'm anybody's." Barbara immediately regretted saying that; it was too early in her relationship-building to be saying things like that. It was cheap, and it was already too late to revise it. The remark was pounced on.

"Can I get you a gin and tonic?" pleaded Maddison

She blushed; she felt her face heat. She, of course, refuse, but was aware that it had been many years since the blood vessels in her face had seen such an influx of blood.

All in attendance laughed it off.

"What time do you like to turn in, Barbara? I mean, do you require assistance at all? We always like to look by and make sure that all meds have been taken and that you are comfortable." A genuine enquiry from her red-haired carer. Barbara had never bothered about what time she went to bed. If there was something good on telly, she would watch it; if not she would go to bed as early as nine o'clock. What business was it of theirs what time she went to bed, she thought? But of course, she was being 'cared' for now.

"Well, I don't know," she replied, "I mean, what happens here in the evenings, do I sit in my room and watch television, or am I expected down here in the lounge?"

"Your call." Barbara was getting fed up with everything being 'her call'; it was obviously the 'in phrase' round here.

"We would welcome female company down here in the evenings," said Ron.

Barbara looked at Ron, almost studying him. He had white hair, sad-looking cow-type eyes, but his bone structure was still visible and Barbara imagined when he was younger he could have been quite handsome. By this time Pinky, who seemed older than the others, had nodded off, and Brian had opened his copy of the Sun.

"Lunch is served."

Barbara had to admit she liked that - she had done nothing towards it and she didn't have to wash up if she didn't want to. Yes, she liked that bit. Pinky obviously found it difficult to feed himself; many of his peas missed their target completely, but then, as Barbara informed the staff later, even the Queen forbids peas to be served to her at a public dinner. But the bit she didn't like was that she felt overwhelmed by the males, and she was somewhat relieved when one by one they wandered off, and that another carer came to move Pinky, who seemed to only be able to walk with assistance, over to a comfy chair in the lounge. He went to sleep again within several minutes. She was left at the table with Ron, who she felt she could handle while he was on his own.

Ron turned out to be an ex-Naval Officer. His wife had died just a year ago, and like so many kids, his believed he would be better off in a home than on his own. He was still not sure, but he saw the arrival of Barbara was promising to change that.

"So far," he told her, "the meals here have been fabulous, and the idea of wine with every meal seems very civilised to me, but between you and me, Barbara ..." He leaned towards her looking around for others who may listen, but there were none. "I think they have a bit of a problem with this Jock business."

"Oh, really?"

"Oh yes, see, it's part of their philosophy here that you can do what you want, and they offer no supervision whatsoever. All very well whilst we all have our marbles, but of course old Jock was losing his, and they let him have *that bottle of Scotch to himself, and he drank the bloody lot, and took those bloody pills. I reckon it was all too much for his heart."*

"What pills?" Barbara asked.

"Viagra."

"What? Look, I keep hearing about this pill, in fact people keep making jokes about it, but I am going to be honest, I don't really know what it is."

Ron realised he had perhaps gone down a cul de sac here, and was left without a choice but to explain to her.

"Well, it's a pill that, shall we say, puts lead back in the pencil."

Barbara looked at him blankly; she was a bit bewildered. She had never heard they saying. Ron elaborated. "It's for men."

She was still nonplussed, her face still searching for understanding by offering a questioning frown towards him.

"Oh, good Lord." He sounded exasperated: he had no choice, "It gives men an erection."

Her jaw dropped open. Ron was fairly certain she knew what he was talking about now.

Eventually she said a "Oh ... but why are they used in here? I mean there would seem to be little need in here for that."

Barbara was a child of the 60s, so now she was on track, she was able to handle it, or so she thought.

"Ah, I think he just wanted to test it with some porn on the internet, but now of course that could all change!" Ron grinned

"What you mean?" asked Barbara

"You!"

The penny dropped. This was blatant; it was so unsubtle, she thought. Her head went to pieces; she had not been in a situation like this for many a year, in fact sex had not even crossed her mind for years, and now here it was in its raw form pushed in front of her. She needed to close it down; she had no intention of indulging in such activity, especially with this lot.

"In your dreams. Look, the loss of my husband was devastating. He meant everything to me. The physical contact was important, but that was because it was him. He cannot be replaced on a whim." It was an old response but always a good one. She decided to back that up by moving from the table, with the excuse that she needed to unpack some things and sort her room out.

It had been in a way a baptism of fire for Barbara: here she was at seventy-two being propositioned. Surely he didn't 'fancy' her? But he did. At supper he apologised for being crude. She was relieved - there was an element of a gentleman in him, and it allowed her to end her first day without too many issues.

Over the next few days Ron pursued her, and she found herself liking his company. He did indeed drive her to the pool for her swimming, and he had joined her in the exercise. Unlike Maddison, who would have created a tsunami should he have dived in, Ron was carrying little weight. In fact she thought, he looked quite good for his age, even though the hairs on his chest were white and grey. She was feeling good with him, and over the days she had learned to deal with the others.

Sue had rung her every day, and Mum had told her she had a friend.

"Perhaps another woman will move in next," Sue had suggested, hoping to make Mum feel less oppressed. But Mum's own reaction surprised even herself. The thought of another woman was not that pleasant. These were her boys now, particularly Ron, and she didn't want competition thank you. What on earth is going on, she thought? Did Ron actually mean something to her?

It was at supper that evening that 'your call girl', the red-haired Scots lady appeared and spoke to Barbara.

"You seem to have settled in well. How do you feel?"

"Well, so far so good."

"Good. You seem to have struck up a friendship with Ron."

Barbara went on the defensive. "There's nothing in it - we are just friends."

"Oh, what a shame. You should get in there, girl, enjoy life while you can." She winked and left.

Ron and Barbara eventually used a Viagra to pursue activity that she thought was well since ended. Both were out of practice but they were mature enough to talk about that, and after several days rehearsing, Barbara let go.

Sue commented that her mother looked really good, her skin had somehow taken on a sheen that Sue had not seen for years. She was smiling, and she cuddled Pinky and Brian, she got them tea, she got them drinks, and she would have even cuddled Madison if she could have got her arm around him. This was everything that Sue could have dreamed about, Mum was happy.

Robert was in the office with his red-headed assistant, along with some official looking individuals. Several official looking women were also walking about the home. Jock's death had not just been ignored, Social Services had something to get their teeth into.

It was just three weeks before Mum, Brian, Pinky, Maddison and Ron were packed and ready to leave for new accommodation. Social services were sorting them out, but Barbara was distraught. Ron was going to a different home.

She was in love with him, but social services needed them to marry before they would consider keeping them together.

There was no wine, no pills, no car, no fun in her new home, but most of all, no Ron.

At the end, Ken was touched by the story. He had become really engrossed in it and had lost all track of time, and all sense of what was going on around him. Until he heard:

"Ken, Ken, come on we're going."

He looked around to see his group making their way towards the pontoon.

"Oh OK, oh crikey, hang on a minute."

He looked around. Where was his girl, the baby's mother? Surely she should be back by now? Where the hell was she?

He couldn't just leave the child here, unattended - that would be criminal.

"Look, what's the matter now? We're just about to board to complete the operation."

"Well … actually at the moment, I'm looking after this baby."

"What!" exclaimed Olly, who had assumed the responsibility for 'discipline' owing to the state of Hardy.

"What do you mean you are looking after a baby?"

"Well I appear to have been left with it, Its mother has gone to change her tampon."

Even more incredulous, Olly was lost for words. Equally the others looked slightly bewildered.

"She asked me to look after it while she went to the loo, but that must have been a good ten minutes ago, and now I cant' see her at all," he said looking desperately around the gardens and promenade.

Hardy had lost the initial flush and now thought he was sober.

"Look, it's not Ken's fault is it, he's just doing a favour for the girl, reaching out across the great divide of generations. The hand of friendship should never be rejected," he added.

"Oh bloody hell, he gets like this when he's had a few." Joyce reinforced what was apparently obvious to all present.

"What we going to do then? We can't just leave the child here," Sarah interjected.

This was apparently dawning on all of them. They would just have to wait until she came back.

"What if she doesn't?" Kenneth enquired.

"Then it's a police job, isn't it?" Olly was straight to the point. This had all the potential of being really serious.

"Oh for goodness sake, we don't want that, I am sure she will be back in a minute." Ken sought to comfort the group.

"You want to read this - she's just given it to me."

"Oh what a great idea," Joyce butted in. "Let's all sit down and have a read in the sunshine, and my husband can get his thick head down then as well." There was obvious sarcasm in her voice, as well as annoyance. They were about to miss yet another ferry while they waited for a mother to change her tampon.

Hardy drawled:

"To say today is not going well would be wrong, you know. Several good things have already come out of it but sadly you're still here, Joyce."

She ignored him; she mostly ignored him, sober or drunk, she ignored him.

There was within the group genuine frustration now. This was the closest they had got to actually pulling off their operation since the abortive attempt earlier in the day. They were aware that it was now nearly four hours since the operation was meant to start, and that these seemingly unavoidable delays were conspiring against them.

But this one was different. This one had all the hallmarks of being serious.

"Well, did she tell you her name or anything?" Olly enquired.

"Not really."

"What do you mean, not really? She either told you or didn't."

"Well, she was in a bit of a rush I think, when she went off."

"Do you know the name of this child?"

"I think she told me, but I don't remember, I know it's about a year old."

"Oh good, we know its age but not its name. Great! And you are left with it."

The others stood there listening without comment to this exchange.

"Is it still asleep?" asked Sarah.

"At the moment yes. Look, I am sure she will be back any minute, why are you all panicking?" Ken now was expressing his hopes rather than the reality of the situation.

"Because we want to get on with this, you dozy sod, and this baby thingy is threatening everything. I mean if we do have to call the police, we are going to have to disappear, we can't all be found here together - they will ask what we are doing."

"They're going to ask Ken that anyway, aren't they?" Sarah interrupted, beginning to feel for her 'friend with benefits'.

"Well three, four, even ten minutes isn't going to make that much difference now is it? I mean we have been farting about since nine this morning, and it's now, what, two o'clock. Don't get on at me, I've been ready to go since this morning, and I am sure this very responsible young lady will be back any minute now."

Kenneth had been reading the piece.

"I'm impressed," he eventually said, lifting his head from the pages.

"Impressed with what?" Olly snapped.

"Hey, let's do peace eh?" Hardy attempted to calm matters.

"Oh, I'll wear a bloody flower in my hair as well, shall I?" Joyce was still furious. "He always reverts to the 60s when he's like this," she informed the whole group.

"This story Ken gave me, it's really good. Did this girl write it?"

"Yes, well that's what she said. It's a true story, apparently, or so she tells me, it was her brother's home."

"Is it a boy or girl?" asked Sarah, again showing that she had given birth and Joyce hadn't. These were the sort of questions a mother would ask.

"Oh, I think it's a boy – not sure, could be a girl."

"Ken, you don't know that either, do you?" Olly was getting more and more frustrated.

"Shouldn't we find out then?" Sarah thought this to be important.

"Oh yes, what another great idea? Why don't we, as a group of old age pensioners, all gather round the pushchair and take the child's trousers down, in full gaze of the general public. Have you thought what that looks like, Sarah?"

No, Sarah had not thought what it looked like. Why would she? She had not the faintest idea of public perception. She was concerned for the child's welfare.

"Look, Sarah, this is the two thousands, not the nineteen hundreds, things have changed. When it comes to kids, no one trusts anyone ever since that Ester Rants stirred things up. I propose that we give her another five minutes to return - we won't get this ferry, which is just returning from Portsmouth, but we need to get on the next one. If she doesn't return, it's off, this is much more important than what we are proposing to do. This is an abandoned child as far as I am concerned, and we will have no choice other than to inform the police."

There was a silence. They all knew deep down that Olly was right, if, and it was still a big if, this turned out to be an abandoned child, then that superseded everything else.

"It's highly unlikely," argued Ken. "She seemed to me like a very responsible young lady, and she took a real interest in elderly people which is obvious if you read her story, which is apparently true as I keep telling you. I am sure she will be back any minute now, with a very good reason for taking a longer time."

"If she doesn't come back, do you reckon you could you describe her to the police, Ken?" Olly asked.

"Um, well I could make a stab at it."

"More likely you could describe her legs and breast size." Joyce was both rude and on form. She knew Ken, she had often said to Hardy: he was in her opinion a letch, always undressing women with his eyes. She had said to Hardy that she often felt that his eyes were stripping her bit by bit, explaining to Hardy how Ken was imagining her breasts falling from her undone bra, and that's not acceptable these days. Hardy had merely agreed.

Ken decided to ignore Joyce, which was the best thing to do when she was in a mood like this. And to be fair, Ken thought, she had every right to be cross, Hardy was hardly fit to be a leader at this moment, and not for the first time in their marriage had drink played a part, he guessed.

There was no option but to agree with Olly. Sarah noticed that the sun had got round to the child, so she eased carefully the pushchair away from the sun so the shade was on the child again. It stirred.

"Oh, bloody hell, what did you do that for?" asked Ken.

"Sun is dangerous, the last thing you want is for this little one to get sunburn - that sun is really strong."

The child started to murmur, it opened its eyes, and for those who have parented it was blatantly obvious it was going to start to grizzle. It had woken up in a bad mood.

The group peered at the child; the child peered at this group of strange faces. They were not beautiful like its mother's face: there were lines all over their faces, there were dark shadows and bits hanging off. And they all looked as if they didn't know what to do. There was only one thing a child of that age could do when confronted with such a situation: yell, and yell loud.

There was slight panic. But Ken remained calm, demonstrating as he thought to the others, that he was in charge of the situation.

"Apparently there is a bottle in the bag at the back. She told me to give it a drink if it woke up."

Sarah went to the bag. Indeed there was a full travelling kit in it with spare nappy, drink and a half drunken bottle of vodka.

"Mm," she muttered, "reliable you say, Ken?"

"Well you don't have a clue about why that is in there, it could be her husband's or something." Ken felt defensive: he had to, because otherwise it made him look really foolish being taken in. Foolish was the word that was already crossing the lips of the group. How could a man of his age get involved in something like this?

Sarah, irritated, thrust the bottle into the child's mouth.

The child fought it; this was not what it wanted, it simply wanted its mother.

This was going to create another conference, but very different from the jovial first conference of the day. All players were fraught, even Sarah was cross with her Ken that he had been so foolish as to believe a stranger with a baby, Joyce cross that Hardy was somewhat close to the wind, Kenneth that he wouldn't get home to his wife because of yet another infernal delay, Ken that he was being accused of being foolish by everyone except Hardy, Olly that he was now responsible, and he had never been good with people, and Hardy, well to be honest, he was actually OK.

From nowhere, the child got its wish. Mum appeared. She had a man in tow as well, perhaps the father.

"Hello baby, mummy's here." She undid the restraining straps and got the child out of the pushchair. The yelling stopped immediately.

"Sorry guys, I had to go up the road to Boots. I hope I haven't held you up too much."

A loud snore was emitted from the bench next to them. It was of course Hardy, who had now reached the stage where the alcohol had taken over his brain function completely. His liver was working like mad to clear his system of the poison he had ingested, and required rest, and in the warm soporific sunshine, Hardy had given in and was now some place else. All knew he was not going to be there for long as Joyce looked over to him. Her disgusted look was on display.

"No, of course not, not at all, there has been no problem," Ken informed her on both his behalf and the group. Olly was not so sure. He was cross that she would wander off like that, but then she had no idea what they had planned so in her head, he supposed, what was ten minutes to pensioners? He tossed up whether to say anything, but for one of the few times in his life he decided not to. Let's just call this another incident, he thought, and let's move on.

"Loved the story – you must give me your email or telephone number. I would love to talk further about that great concept."

"Look Ken, we need to get going."

"Yes yes, I know. This will only take a few seconds. You lot wake him up and go on, I'll catch you up," he said, pointing to Hardy.

Joyce was cruel: she leant over Hardy and pinched his cheek - there was plenty of loose flesh to grab. It looked hard and aggressive, taking the violence between them to another level, thought the others.

Ken got the girl's name and email. Her name was vaguely familiar but he couldn't immediately place it.

CHAPTER 9

Bert returned to his kitchen table; two empty old, but classy brandy glasses now rested on the surface. There was a small pool of some liquid, isolated like an island in a sea. The now-departed Hardy's empty glass rested close by the pool of liquid. Bert was unsure of whether it was brandy on the table, or just water from condensation. He put his finger into it. and tasted the tip of his finger - sure enough it was brandy, probably when he had missed the glass pouring more for Hardy. He got a cloth to wipe it, and with some almost amusement noted that in the short time the brandy had rested on the wooden surface, it had started to remove the French polish leaving a paler area which would permanently remind him of this fleetingly happy time.

"Good God," he said to himself, 'if it does that to polish, what does it do to a person's insides?" He looked at the marks on the table and reflected that the visit by Hardy had indeed been refreshing and pleasant. In fact it had been a major event for him. When was the last time he had sat and drank with a friend, particularly in his own home? He could not remember any time. Yes, he had partaken of the odd glass of sherry round the vicarage after church every first Sunday in the month, but somehow that seemed artificial.

Until recently the characters at that event seemed to be cut out of cardboard, all being pleasant. Now, however, the characters were showing signs of life.

This cancer stuff scared Bert - why wouldn't it, he thought? He was entitled to be scared, but on top of being scared, he faced the problem of not being able to share that fear with anyone.

Bert made what was for him a reckless decision: he poured another brandy, leaving just about an inch in the bottle, and then he would have a sleep, he told himself. The tiredness came over him like a wave as he gulped - not sipped but gulped the glass he had poured for himself. It was a different taste from earlier, or felt like it. The brandy had represented companionship, natter and the sharing of thoughts. Now his companion was gone, the brandy somehow tasted different.

Bert reflected on the past hour. He had been amazed at how Hardy had loosened up with the effects of the fourth bucket of brandy. Bert looked at the bottle that had been nearly full when Hardy had arrived - it was now sporting about an inch in the bottom. Surely Hardy had grabbed a quick one while he had gone to the toilet? Bottles never tell lies, he thought.

Bert had not been prepared for the disclosures about Hardy's private life.

Hardy had said to Bert that he was best off not being married. Even back when you're young, what did marriage actually do, Hardy had asked? He had gone on to answer the question himself: "It keeps you bloody captive, that's what Bert. You have a contract with this woman to remain true and loyal to her for the rest of your bloody life, Bert, and the thing is, back in the days when this bloody marriage thingy was set up, you only lived until you were thirty something. You didn't have to put up with fifty sodding years of the same woman. I mean, don't get me wrong, Bert, it's the same for the women as well; you both grow apart over such a long period of time, mate. I'm sure us humans were never designed for such monogamy."

To a certain degree, even though semi-incoherently, Hardy was reinforcing Bert's shallow understanding of relationships, but it had provoked Bert into a question. He thought now he could ask such things because he was getting close to Hardy - you get close with alcohol.

"But surely," he asked in all innocence, "you would miss the company, and I assume stuff like cuddling and sex?"

Under normal circumstances, Hardy would have been taken aback by the intimacy of the question, but his 'aback' sensations had been well and truly dulled.

"Maybe early on, but when you grow apart everything disappears. I can't remember the last time I 'banged' Joyce, and cuddles just don't happen any more, Bert. Company, well yes, in a way. She is there, and that is about all you can say, and I guess it still has to be better than an empty house."

"Tell me about it," replied Bert. "I talk to myself and I get no reply. I sometimes get frightened that there is no one there to do silly things like call an ambulance should I pass out or something. I mean Joyce would do that, wouldn't she?"

"Most likely I guess." Hardy had thought about it a bit longer and offered further confirmation. "Yeah, I am pretty certain she would."

Bert's normal reticence had left him, "Shame about the sex stuff. You must miss it." It was more a question than a statement.

"Did a few years back, but you know yourself, you see a

gorgeous-looking woman nowadays, and you know you fancy them, but have a job remembering why. I mean to be frank, Bert, if that weather girl with the big tits came in the room now and stripped off, would either of us be able to do much about it?"

Bert had not known. He had never really thought about it, and on top of that it wasn't going to happen anyway.

"We still sleep together, but that is what it is … sleep. In a way, she's weird because she says she don't like me, well it may even be worse than that, she may even be despise me, yet the soppy cow sometimes still undresses in front of me. I don't know whether this is a sort of … almost saying 'look at this, but you ain't getting anywhere near it, sunshine'. If it is that, then it ain't working. I mean, Bert, those bra's she wears are a miracle of engineering. They hold up an equivalent of a five-pound bag of spuds in each pocket and when they are released at night, it is like the Dam Busters' bombs being dropped all over again. They reach her ferking navel, Bert, they could knock you out, mate."

Even in his inebriated state, Bert had been unsure that this was the sort of conversation he should be having. It was becoming quite distasteful and in modern parlance 'too much information'. Bert had needed to send Hardy on his way, and pointed this out to him.

"Hardy old chap, don't forget your mission today, as nice as this is, I think you should look to return to the troops."

"You're right, Bert." Bert noticed that the old wooden chair, with very worn leather seats had become difficult for Hardy to move, for no other reason than Hardy was finding it difficult to move himself.

Bert now thought that the last brandy had been a mistake, and somehow he knew that 'she' would spot that Hardy had been drinking when he got back to the ferry.

Once more on his own, Bert was now getting near to feeling drunk, and he wondered what effect this was all going to have on his body when taken in conjunction with the cocktail of pills he was prescribed. He was, however, now not really caring that much: he had a new friend and perhaps the two of them could have chats like that afternoon again.

He had no brothers or sisters; his nearest relative was a cousin who he had not seen in years. He had once been quite close to her, but thinking about it, she could now even be dead – would anyone have thought to tell him? He doubted it; his name did not appear in many address books. His cousin Frieda had moved away from Gosport many years ago, having become the wife of a Salvation Army Officer. Just like the 'real' army they were posted to different regions and jobs every two or three years.

He thought about her now - Harriet, her name was, wasn't it? No, he had just thought it was Frieda, but he revised his thinking - he was sure it was Harriet now. Perhaps he was thinking more clearly now that the brandy was getting into his system. Thinking hard, he remembered the last time he had seen her, which must have been twenty years ago, when he had attended his aunt's seventieth birthday celebrations. She was then around forty, he guessed, and a real live wire, full of life and love for everyone. Her husband did not strike Bert as a Salvation Army Officer type: he had a belly on him that any beer drinker would be proud of, so the sin of alcohol had obviously been replaced with gluttony.

At the end of the party, when others were drifting away and his mother was engaged in conversation with her sister, Harriet had come and sat with her Cousin Bert. He felt it strange that another adult should address him as 'cousin' but she appeared to prefer it that way, even though it seemed so old fashioned and more at home in a period drama on the telly. She had asked all the normal things about work, his health and his love life. What an odd question he thought: in fact it was an invasive and challenging question, and probably on reflection one that his busy-body mother had probably asked her to ask.

She didn't wait particularly for an answer, and moved onto even heavier stuff.

"I mean, Cousin Bert, that there must be lots of ladies out there just longing to meet a nice guy like you. And its easy nowadays; lots of agencies out there that match you up with women actually seeking relationships."

It provided a theme to his daydreams that had lasted many years, yet he had done nothing about it very much. She told him of some of the stuff she had done in training, about being aware of self worth. She too was a Salvation Army Officer and her training had taken her into all sorts of subject matter related to the human spirit. She told him of a book she had been told to read, 'The Empty Raincoat' by Charles Handy. It was the story of a rich man who made lots of money in the Far East. He had seldom visited his father and it wasn't until he found himself flying back home to Ireland where his father, a protestant vicar, was reported to him as being seriously ill, that he realised his lack of concern. The son had not made it home in time, and his father had died just before the plane had touched down in Dublin. The son had been too busy making money, dining, drinking and partying generally with his well-connected friends.

His father's funeral was attended by literally hundreds of people, who upon seeing his son approached him with numerous stories of how his father had affected and often changed their lives. His father, with no money, had earned riches beyond belief, a community that loved him for the amount of giving he had achieved in his lifetime. The book had been a prerequisite to her first ever dissertation, entitled 'My funeral, and who will come to it.'

It was, she had told him, a very hard essay to write; it challenged her very reason for being. In the essay, she assumed her mother, who was of course still alive at that point, would come and her husband. The question was whether they would come because they wanted to, or because it was seen as a sense of duty? Bert was astonished - why would she even question such a motive?

Indeed, thought Bert in retrospect, this is an essay that all of us should attempt, and currently he feared it would be a very easy essay for him to write. Whose life had he affected? What good had he brought to the world? Just because one attended church every Sunday made very little difference at all, it's what you did for others, what your actions were for the other days of the week, and in that department he was sadly lacking.

Harriet or Frieda, whatever her name was, had a soothing influence upon him; she seemed to have that ability to make one feel comfortable whatever she said. Not because what she had said was easy - indeed it was challenging - but because everything she said, whilst sometime arguable was never malicious, never aimed and never without care to articulate her argument sensibly and without offence.

He often wondered what it would have been like to have been married to a woman like her, to feel the love of a woman, the tenderness that was brought into a man's life by marriage. And yet he looked at couples like Hardy and Joyce, who seemed in perpetual conflict. And they were not the only ones – he knew of many couples who just seemed to drift along in a habit and in reality should not be together.

His only contact with a woman as a potential girlfriend had been a NAAFI girl when he was in the RAF. He had asked her out after days of nervous anticipation of rejection. But she agreed to go for a drink in the local pub. The date had been a disaster. Upon arrival, the girl seemed to know every person in the bar and spent time talking to them. She did eventually join him, where he had bought the customary Babycham for her. "Is there any brandy in it?" she had asked. There wasn't. This was obviously a disappointment to the girl. He had run out of conversation after just five minutes, and found the whole situation stressful. It got worse when he got back to his mess.

"Did you get your leg over then, Bert?"

He hadn't.

But it seemed like all the other men in the mess had. He would not be doing that again in a hurry. The episode had helped feed his inferiority complex, which he had never managed to overcome.

"You only get your leg over if you put a brandy in her Babycham," was the advice.

So, almost a prostitute then, he had thought, not the sort of girl he could take back home. He did have in mind, at that point in his life, his ideal girl. She would be plain but devoted, dress modestly but be sexy with him. She would cook for him, and she would carry a faint scar just to the left of her nose where she had had a wart removed. He would find that endearing.

But alas, he never found her; perhaps he never looked hard enough.

The house had been left to him by his mother when she died. He had been very close to her. He was aware that a few friends and family had thought the relationship unhealthy because of the closeness, be it right or wrong,

Bert had never really felt the need to seek any relationship outside the family home. Mother cooked for him, cleaned the house, made his bed, did his washing and took hardly any money for it. All Bert had to do was to go to work, to a workplace that he could walk to, where he knew everyone and knew his job backwards. It was only later that he realised that he had got into a 'rut'.

Did he regret that? No, he thought. Having seen the disasters of other marriages he sometimes breathed a sigh of relief that he was not involved with such mayhem, and Hardy's visit was almost a vitally important verification of that opinion and choice of lifestyle.

Bert was aware that there had been talk in his family and amongst closer friends of the family as to whether he was gay. He hated that word; it was a word that had been hijacked and very often incorrectly. He had met 'gays' who were far from what the term indicated - indeed they lived a life bordering on misery and Bert thought that was unfair. They had every right to a decent life the same as anyone else, and so what did it matter if he was 'gay'? He was not, however – indeed he wondered whether he was what he thought they called 'asexual', just not interested in sex. He had never knowingly leered at anyone. He would find bikini-clad ladies on the beach attractive in the main, but in his view this was often spoiled, he thought, by some women wearing such a garment who quite frankly should not.

So it looked like he would now go to his grave without having experienced the love of a woman partner. But he had experienced many more years than most of the love of his mother. Unhealthy it may have been, but he felt happy with it. It was a different 'love' to be sure, but one that asked no questions and told no lies. She knew him backwards and inside out, and he felt pretty much the same about her. The thing was that always niggled him a bit was that he knew very little about her life before she had met dad; in fact she was almost silent on the subject, but he had always reasoned she was entitled to a little mist of mystery.

Bert's biggest fear was having to go into a nursing home. He had never been the most social animal and the thought of having to mix with others, often smelly and confused others, filled him with dread. Just sitting around a room all day, waiting like in the doctor's, only this time the waiting room for death. No matter how jolly the staff, no matter how bright the decoration, no matter what 'stimulants' were provided by well-meaning owners or charities, in Bert's mind there was no getting away from the exact nature of the homes: "God's waiting room."

Since he had been diagnosed with cancer, his doctor had suggested involving Social Services, and perhaps he would like to think about whether he would be better off in a decent care facility. Bert would have the money to pay: he could sell his home and be able to pay for the best care, which often could come in at over eleven hundred pounds per week. If he achieved one hundred and seventy thousand for the house, he would be able to pay for at least one hundred and fifty weeks, and then, when his savings were depleted, the council would step in and assist in payment.

Bert had asked the burning question: would he actually need to pay for as long as three years? The doctor had been frank and frankly doubted it. He had lots of cash stashed away in various building societies. He had earned an adequate salary during his working life but had never spent it. Indeed, he didn't even spend his income now.

So the decision to sell his house was one that was on the radar, and he had said to himself that he needed time to come to terms with this. This was a huge step and one which he thought both the doctor and Social Services seemed to treat as just another financial transaction. In his mind it was much more important than that: basically Bert saw it as giving up your place on the planet, so in common with so many other people facing the same questions, he 'kicked the can down the road'. This place had been his home all his life. Yes it was dark and dingy, but it had in its time been full of love and happiness, and he could relate to that as he sat there.

Bert had never been one to complain; he went along with what the 'authorities' said. He believed the BBC. The BBC was his source of information along with the local newspaper which he now purchased infrequently, mainly because of the price and secondly because he was fed up with reading about a bleeding heart that had somehow been deprived of something, and the paper thought it was a good cause. 'No they didn't' he would think. 'They think it will sell the paper, and they are miles off beam.' The BBC, however, was starting to annoy him for the simple reason that they would start a news item and then cut it short saying that the full information could be gained on the BBC website. Bert was not connected to the internet. He was scared of it and had persuaded himself that he did not need it. He could do what he needed with his bank by going into the branch, and the nice people in there would just sort things out for him. And then further, he argued, again with himself, that all these scam things and fraud on the internet, he could do without, thank you.

"I have some sympathy with you," Hardy had told Bert one Sunday morning when discussing the issue over sherry, "and you are not alone. Do you know, I was reading the other day that there are more than twelve million people who lack the skills to take advantage of the internet thingy?

Even three out of every ten people over the age of sixty-five do not use the internet, and I hate to think of the numbers falling behind in things like digital payment methods."

"Well in some ways," Bert had replied, "it's good to know I am not alone."

"You should go into the library, Bert," Hardy suggested to him. "They run simple introduction courses for people like you. See, I think it's just fear – you're frightened of the unknown like we all are but once it's explained to you I think you would enjoy it." Bert had not been convinced and remained one of the thousands of people in this country who were disenfranchised by not being able to compete in competitions, denied news coverage, denied sometimes cheaper prices because offers only existed on line.

But sitting there now, a little soaked in brandy, it seemed not to matter one jot. It didn't matter because he soon would not exist, and the percentage of those not connected to this 'new' world would be reduced by a fraction of a point. The statistics would read just that little bit better without the Government having to lift a finger.

Bert was beginning to feel quite unwell. He put it down to the fact that he had had too much brandy, and his observation of the level of drink left in the bottle confirmed that. He would, he thought, take himself off to bed and sleep it off for the rest of the afternoon, and be awake for the return of Hardy with the bulb for his light. The kitchen appeared to be spinning and getting darker. It's got to be the brandy, he reasoned again, but he had never experienced these feelings. He was becoming even more hot and clammy. He was fighting for breath now, with pains in his chest and shoulders. He needed some water, but for some reason his legs did not seem to respond to his wish to get to the sink. He did, however, hear the bang as his head hit the table, but the pain went and all his worries suddenly seemed irrelevant. Earth's vain shadows fled.

CHAPTER 10

The vicar of Christ Church was a shared vicar. He looked after two congregations, the other being Holy Trinity Church, which was nestled between the two tower blocks of flats that had some of the best views in the world. The two congregations 'got on', but that was about all. There was no real 'meeting of minds' mainly because Holy Trinity was 'high' church and Christ Church was best described as middle of the road.

This cuddling business during services was, however, beginning to put Joyce off, and she supposed in her head that she was probably more 'high' than 'low' church. But earlier in the week she had, for the first time in her life, turned to the church for help and advice, as well as to her solicitor. The charity Relate was completely booked up; they had no slots for her until well into next year. That was no good, which she thought was a shame because in all honesty they could have done with seeing both her and Hardy, which would have helped them sort out formal separation issues.

In the last few weeks, Hardy had seemed genuinely unhappy and that had surprised her. The vicar had agreed to see her, and she decided that he was as good a sounding board as any.

He was a man in his early fifties she estimated, though it was difficult to age him because his hair was still jet black, but plastered with some hair grease and swept backwards. He was what she thought of as slightly portly, but a NHS routine medical would probably say he was obese.

He had greeted her at the door of the vicarage and looked around for Hardy who he was obviously expecting to be with her.

"No Hardy today, then?"

"No, well actually that is why I am here."

She was surprised that he was totally astounded when she told him of her plans to divorce Hardy. The pair of them had obviously not given much away to the 'public'.

"I have to say," he said, "that I am somewhat taken aback. I mean everyone knows the two of you argue with each other, but I had not thought of it as being anything more than petty stuff, and that underneath it all the relationship was built on rock. Well, I am so sorry to hear that I was wrong. On the other hand, of course, I may not be wrong. It may be that you are so close to the issues that you cannot see what others see."

Joyce frowned at that.

"Sorry, what do 'others' see? I'll tell you what they don't see, what goes on behind the closed doors of hell." Joyce had raised her voice, and had become animated.

A bit dramatic, thought the vicar, even by Joyce's standards.

The vicar's wife tapped on the door. She entered without being bid, a small very delicate woman, carrying a tray with two mugs of tea, some milk and sugar and a few shortbread biscuits on a plate, which she placed on the small table, the table that formed a barrier to hide behind.

The wife said little, just a polite 'hello' to Joyce, and got out of the room very quickly after she had received a "thank you love, leave the door ajar will you?" from the vicar.

Joyce noticed the 'leave the door' bit: these days even vicars had to be careful, she supposed.

"Help yourself to milk and sugar, and do have a biscuit."

The arrival of the tea had the effect of taking some of the heat out of Joyce. She had been irritated with the 'what people see' remark. She wanted to get over to him the sheer hell of the relationship as she saw it, and whilst pouring milk into her tea she continued:

"I can do absolutely nothing without some sort of snide comment. And he is just so boring these days." What had she just said, she asked herself in her head? That was pathetic and in no way reflected the true position. Indeed, the vicar picked up on it; she had failed to make her case.

"But neither of those things are a reason to break up a marriage, Joyce, and I am going to be quite frank here - if you came here today hoping for some spiritual approval to divorce, then you are not going to get it. I am afraid that I believe marriage is for life and when things go wrong, you should work at it. What I can offer," he continued, "is for us to pray together and to ask God for spiritual guidance, and to shine his light on the pathways open to both of you."

"Um, no I don't think so." Joyce found the situation developing into something embarrassingly personal. She had never before been in a position of being invited to pray with someone except in the formal backdrop of the church, as part of the congregation. She didn't like it and it could, in the worst scenario she thought, lead to those 'cuddles' that this vicar seemed so keen on, a development that she wished to avoid.

She was, she thought to herself, in the wrong place, but she was going to have to listen to more as the vicar continued. He had picked up that the prayer thing was not going to happen and moved on.

"So I'd like to explore more with you whether you actually understand all the implications regarding what you are proposing. I mean, for example, have you have looked at where you are going to live? That's probably one of the biggest things."

"Well, I reckon it's that subject which is getting Hardy so upset. Obviously we will have to sell up and split stuff. I fully realise that I am probably going to have to rent, or buy one of those caravan things. I'm less concerned about ownership than Hardy is – he seems obsessed by it."

"It is a man-thing I think, the need to provide a castle, but there's nothing wrong with that." He took a sip of tea, and Joyce decided to take a biscuit after all. They had somehow worked on her, staring at her from the plate and working away at her resolve to ignore them.

"Whatever it is, I think it is the threat of having to sell up that is really upsetting him and not the fact that we are separating." As she said that, she realised that a shortbread crumb left her mouth on the 'p' of separating. The vicar ignored it, a true gentleman. She thought how different he was to Hardy, who would have made a real fuss about it and tried to embarrass her.

"It's interesting, Joyce, how you keep deflecting emotion onto Hardy. I have asked several times what you think about having to sell up, about things like splitting money, furniture and – most of all – the memories, yet you keep telling me how you think Hardy is coping and what he is thinking. Now tell me about you, please. For example, will you stay in Gosport?"

What a strange question, she thought.

"Of course I will."

"Why? The world is your oyster, apart from the issues of cost."

She could see what he was trying to do: a new life, one where she would be free. This was quite clever, she thought, because she could see that his real aim was to provoke her.

"Well, all my friends are …" she trailed off. What friends? Yes she knew people from the church, but real friends in whom she could confide about problems like this were thin on the ground. In fact they were nowhere on the ground. She had changed tack.

"I like it here, I love the sea, and there is a very long coastline around here. There is always something going on in the Harbour, and we have things like the Discovery Centre, which is brilliant. I will be able to make friends in places like that once I have got away from Hardy. He holds me back, you know, stops me chatting to people, always pokes his nose into my conversations with people. He'll have one hell of a job finding company; he can't hold a conversation, you know. All you get is one-liners, short statements. It drives you up the wall when you want to talk."

The vicar, aware that Joyce had yet again transferred the object of the conversation to Hardy, ignored it this time he asked, "So you will rent in Gosport? Have you thought of where?"

No she hadn't, but that was not a big problem unless Hardy rented the place next door.

The vicar added, "Look no matter how you dress this up, two individuals at your ages are never going to live as comfortably as one couple does." He was beginning to sound like her solicitor. "Rent will soon eat away at your capital until you qualify for Housing Benefit."

Housing Benefit! Housing Benefit! That would mean

going to the Council and the other Social Security places. That would mean having to sit and wait with others, which she did not fancy one little bit. She was sure it would never come to that.

"Unless," the vicar continued, "you find yourself another relationship. Would you want to?"

"To be honest I have not given it much thought. At this moment in time I doubt it very much. You don't get rid of one bundle of trouble to substitute it with another, do you?"

The vicar viewed that as a rhetorical question and did not reply.

"One of the issues surrounding silver divorce," he said, "is loneliness. You may not appreciate it, but the very fact that Hardy is in the house, and says little things to you during the day means that the feeling of isolation is less prevalent."

At this, her hackles rose. She was not hearing what she wanted to hear: this was, in her opinion, coming from a male perspective.

"It is possible to be lonely in a marriage, you know. I mean whatshername said that." 'Whatshername' suddenly came to her so she added, "Princess Diana."

"Oh, yes, I accept that, but is it the same loneliness you experience when nobody is in the house? Nobody on those dark winter nights, nobody to cuddle up to."

The vicar seemed to be going off on one, she thought.

"The warmth of another body in the bed, the comfort of arms, the comforting aroma of your partner giving you that sense of love."

"Look have you not heard a word of what I have said? We sleep in single beds, I have not felt his arms around me for years, and as for the aroma of a loved one, yes you are quite right, I will miss the smell of his farting after sprouts, baked beans, Guinness and goodness knows what else."

"Sorry, I got a bit carried away there, I mean in lots of ways I was thinking as much about myself as about you, and that is terribly unprofessional."

"Were you?" she replied, surprised.

"Yes, Margaret and I are not what it seems you know - we have our problems too."

"I'd have never thought it."

"Sorry, we are not here to discuss Margaret and myself, this is about you."

She could do nothing else but agree, even though her interest had been aroused. He continued:

"Have you explored any way you could live in the same property, sort of co existing with each other but to all effects living separate lives? That way, your finances would remain intact and your security would be better."

"That sounds fine, " she replied, "but how does it work in reality? We do have a spare bedroom, which I have suggested several times that he move into and he won't. How does it work with food? How does it work in the evenings with one lounge? And what about Sundays – does he sit it a different place in church to me, starting gossip? Things like who does the cleaning, who pays for the electricity, even down to changing a light bulb. There seems to be so many problems with that."

"Well, I do know couples that live in the same property, almost as separate flats."

Joyce was aware that the vicar had shifted positions and was suggesting ways in which they might be able to move forward without the huge trauma that would ensue from selling the house, splitting the furniture, changing bank accounts and telling the various agencies. They would also avoid paying out legal fees. It was going down the same line as her solicitor, but Joyce still saw enormous problems, and the biggest one was going to be Hardy's attitude to the whole thing.

"Has Hardy suggested anything like that?" the vicar asked after a few seconds of silence.

She chimed in with a dismissive: "No, I don't think he has thought anything about it. In fact I think sometimes he doesn't even think it is going to happen. You see, this is the problem all the time – he hasn't got any get up and go. He's almost depressive. I mean, he said to me the other day that if he didn't have bad luck, he would have no luck at all. I mean what sort of attitude is that?"

"Did you ever love and admire him?" The vicar's question seemed almost vicious, challenging the basis of the whole marriage. "I'm pretty sure you did, so have you tried to see where things started to go wrong?"

Joyce knew exactly when things went wrong. When she had become aware that Hardy did not give a jot about her, and she related the story of the night she went off with the other guy.

"Honestly, it meant nothing. I was really driven by the thought of getting pregnant."

"It would not have meant nothing if you were asking Hardy to bring up someone else's child, would it? Think how the other chap would have felt if you were having his baby."

"I'd probably have had it terminated. I just wanted to prove that I could get pregnant."

The vicar was not happy at this revelation: this was sin on top of sin to his mind.

"So then, let's be quite straight about this, you committed an act of adultery and would have been quite happy to terminate the life given by God of any baby that resulted from this adultery."

Put like that, she she realised that in his eyes she was just about the worse sinner one could meet. She was not going through any pearly gates, and what's more, analysed in that fashion, for the first time since the event, it gave her a sense of guilt.

"But he didn't care. He didn't as much as roll over in bed when I did get in." She continued to labour her point.

"Perhaps he was cross."

"Then row! Row! That's what I bloody wanted, I wanted him to shout at me, to tell me that I was out of order, and that we needed to sit down and talk about our relationship. I wanted him to tell me that he loved me and he didn't want to lose me and that he would work to keep me, but what did I get? Nothing."

The vicar was somewhat taken aback by the emotion that was now pouring forth, but she wasn't finished, even though she was obviously getting upset.

"I mean, he's said now that he doesn't want a divorce, that it will ruin both of us, but he never says 'Joyce I want to stay with you', does he?"

The vicar was unsure as to how to respond. But it was seeming more and more to him that deep down she just wanted to be loved, and that Hardy had not actually offered that in years. This couple were in a real mess and they did need proper help, which he was uncertain as to whether he was suitably qualified to offer.

"I mean, all the years I have given up for him, working on his business, and for what?"

The vicar didn't know that either.

He took a risk.

"What's the chances of you both coming in?"

"What me and him together?"

"Yes."

"I think that may give him the wrong signals. He may think that I am about to relent."

"Relent? What are you talking about? This isn't about having toad-in-the-hole for tea, this is about your marriage, and the importance of that marriage."

The verb 'relent' had annoyed him. She appeared to have not budged an inch during this conversation. The vicar's opinion was that this whole thing of her wanting a divorce was an absolute disaster, and she should be persuaded to - at least - look at living separately.

"Why don't you put the separate living ideas to Hardy, say for a trial period, and see how it works?"

Joyce was silent, realising that he was not just on one person's side, but in full Christian tradition was trying to compromise.

She would think about it, she told him. He noted that her eyes were watery; he had never ever seen that, but then again why would he have done? He had not known her that well before.

Hardy was in the downstairs toilet when Joyce stormed through the door. The tea she had partaken of at the vicar's had worked its way through, and her need of the toilet was now urgent. In fact it got more urgent as soon as she put the key in the door.

"Oh, for God's sake!" she screamed as she realised the most vital of rooms was occupied.

She would have to try and make it upstairs, bellowing "Bloody man, always doing things to annoy me."

Hardy thought that charge to be a little unreasonable, firstly because he had no idea that she was about to charge through the door, and secondly he had as much right as her to be on the toilet. Several years ago, they had spent rather a lot of money having a second toilet put in downstairs. They had both come to the point whereby when a toilet was needed, it was actually needed now, not in five minutes time, not even in two minutes time, but now. The second toilet had been a Godsend in recent years, even though the building works to have it installed had produced much stress and expense. Neither Hardy or Joyce had ever envisaged that sewers could be so complicated, and that effluent needed so much care and examination by building inspectors. But for Joyce right now to have to go upstairs to the toilet was touch and go … perhaps not the best way to explain it, because it actually became 'go' and a fresh pair of pants were required from the airing cupboard.

Funny thing, women's pants - they say so much about a woman, thought Hardy as he caught her fishing around in the airing cupboard. Joyce had maintained a youthful wardrobe of underwear at least, and had not lapsed into large bloomers that when fluttering on a washing line gave wind direction for incoming aircraft to Southampton Airport. In fact her underwear was actually sexy, and if it didn't hide a bitter twisted and illogical individual he could see how she could still be quite attractive even at her age. She had selected a pair of sky-blue rather skimpy panties to replace the now used green ones. It was an odd sight that greeted Hardy as he climbed the stairs to walk into what was invariably going to be another rollicking. There she was, bottomless, furrowing in the cupboard for some clean pants.

Despite the state of their relationship, she seemed little bothered that he was passing within just a few inches of her now naked backside.

"Why is it that you are always always in my way?"

"Why is it that you have to always repeat 'always'?" was

his rather irrelevant retort.

She ignored it, like she always did.

"I mean, you've had all bloody morning to be in there, and you have to wait until I come back in to park your bum on the loo."

"I didn't know that you were coming back right at that minute, did I? How could I have possibly known your ETA?"

Joyce ignored what for Hardy was quite a logical defence.

Hardy ignored her mood and complaints and went neutral.

"Do you want a cup of tea?"

"No thank you, I had more than enough round the vicarage - in fact that's what probably caused this little accident."

"Good job we got two toilets then, isn't it?"

She'd ignored that. Did she even hear it, Hardy wondered? He was having a cup of tea anyway, and so he reversed on the stairs, passing the naked backside again, only this time giving it a pat with his hand through the banisters.

She'd ignored that too. Indeed, did she even feel it, thought Hardy?

Again, Joyce thought, he hasn't shown any interest in what has just gone on around the vicarage. That made her cross yet again.

"So I assume you discussed all out private stuff with the vicar then?"

Ah, at last she thought - some reaction!

"I wouldn't tell him everything, but we did have a discussion about the way forward."

"The way forward? I thought that was why you had seen your solicitor."

"It was, but he just deals with the legal stuff."

"And when can I expect a letter from him?" asked Hardy.

"When I set things going. I am aware that you have not got yourself one yet."

"I shall use George."

"George?" Joyce produced more of an exclamation than a question.

"Yes, why not? He's looked after us for years."

"Exactly, 'us' being the operative word. You shouldn't put him into the position of having to take sides; you should find someone more neutral.

George was the solicitor the couple had used for years and years while they were running the business. He was a wiry old character, who these days only did the odd job for the practice that he had worked for almost since qualifying.

"Have you asked him yet, because I would be surprised if he wanted anything to do with it?"

"No, I haven't asked him yet. I was thinking of doing it this afternoon. I may give him a ring later."

This apathy she thought, this lack of energy. She wanted to pick Hardy up and shake him, but even with the best will in the world Joyce was defeated there: she would not be strong enough to lift him, let alone shake him.

"So," continued Hardy, "What did you actually talk about? I suppose whatever it was you spent most of the time slagging me off."

"You amaze me. You think I wanted to talk about you? You think you are that important?"

This had all the signs of kicking off yet again, thought Hardy. He decided to end it.

"OK, it is obviously between you and the vicar, so leave it. I don't want to know what you discussed. I suppose at the end of the day it has nothing to do with me, does it?"

"Not really, no. But, well, look." Joyce was hesitant. "There are issues that we should really be discussing, and try and get sorted before any legal battle makes us both broke."

Hardy was surprised at this outbreak of what appeared to him to be common sense. His anxiety was expressed in his next question, which came out as almost pleading.

"Joyce, do you really think that you and I are capable of sitting down and discussing anything without ripping each others heads off?"

"We may need help. The vicar has offered to be a go-between."

"How does that work? You've been round to him for a hour or so this morning and you've no doubt got him on side with you."

"Well, there you go, that's a great start isn't it? You are not even prepared to accept the offer of help from another guy. I thought you would welcome that; he would be seeing things from a male perspective."

"Male? They get all the male hormones removed when they do their training with the church, I reckon."

Could she? No she couldn't, but she couldn't resist; she had to say it.

"So where did you get yours removed then?"

This time however, she actually regretted saying it. It was indeed cruel, and it was almost like she had got into a habit of being cruel, of using every gap unprotected by Hardy as a chance to land a blow. That one remark brought a realization that perhaps it wasn't just Hardy that was the problem. Almost instantly she said:

"Sorry, that was uncalled for."

Hardy found the apology difficult to cope with. He tried to remember when she had last said sorry to him. He drew the cup of tea to his lips, both as a defensive tool and to give him time to think. He remembered the British Prime Minister Harold Wilson - he used a pipe to give him thinking time. When you have something at your lips, he thought, you can't say anything, and others recognise that, so they are not expecting you to say anything.

Joyce thought he had just accepted the apology and moved on, because she could use this interval to inject the realism that was slowly dawning on her as a result of both her visits to her solicitor and vicar.

"He is actually advising that we try living separately in this house. It may need a few tweaks and things to allow that, but I am prepared to give it a go if you are."

The cup remained at Hardy's lips. Events were moving almost too fast to keep up with. The advantage that Joyce had over him, he reasoned, was that she had already sorted things out in her head when she announced the divorce proceedings, and he had not had any time to process the event.

Hardy's mind worked overtime in seconds now, realising that perhaps Joyce had lost that strategic advantage. She had obviously received information that had led her to believe that this divorce thing was not as easy as she imagined. He had been devastated by it and it was true that it was as much the thought of upheaval as not having her around, even though for ninety-five percent of the time they drove each other up the wall.

He was prepared to grasp this easy way out. Eventually, he lowered the cup.

"Oh," was what came out, not really a constructive comment but still buying time. Then he sought further information.

"So how do you see that working then, exactly?"

As usual, she had indeed had the time, albeit short, to think it through.

"Well, put simply, one of us lives upstairs and one lives downstairs. We turn the second bedroom into a lounge-cum-kitchen and we put a shower downstairs. Of course we sleep separately, so one room down here would have to become a bedroom. We would need things like another television and computer, and of course lots of other things, but nowhere near as much as if we actually both moved.

"I know there will be loads of questions, but we would be divorced in all but name. I would be able to live my own life, but we would probably maintain outwardly to others that we were still married, like attending church as a couple, that sort of thing."

"Not that different to how things are at the moment is it, Joyce?"

"Oh, very different. No more touching, like you did just now, no more meals together, no more watching bloody Match of the Day for me, and no months of Strictly Come Dancing for you to endure with me. In fact no more conversations or rows, because apart from essentials we've no need to speak."

This was certainly a better option, and for the moment Hardy was going to go along with it.

"So when does this all start then?"

"Well, we can talk about that. Do you want a corned beef sandwich for lunch? I'll do those fishcakes and chips for tonight."

"Oh … thanks, OK."

Lots of things had been going round in her mind, like could he use the washing machine? Which one of them would do the garden? They need to inform their insurance people. Hot water, electricity, sewage and water supply, central heating – would that all just split in two? Indeed who put the bin out? No doubt things could be worked out.

At the time of this great ferry adventure, Joyce and Hardy's move to living apart had not exactly progressed. They had in fact, during the time between the day of the 'great discussion' and today, done absolutely nothing about it. The rows continued, as did her apparent non-respect of Hardy. She had been marginally impressed with his vision for the operation today, but he had certainly blown that again with the way the day was going and now, waiting for a ferry yet again, she resolved to start things moving back at home, as soon as tomorrow.

The house was spotless. Joyce took great pride in providing a home that was almost sterile. She was a traditionalist, and cooked almost every day except when they ate out, and that was rare. They lived in a house close to the town; it was in an ideal position, whereby they were able to walk to shops and banks, doctor's surgeries and the ferry.

The ferry gave them instant access to another transport hub on the Portsmouth side - vital, because the people of Gosport had no rail link, so the nearest station for them was Portsmouth Harbour. Alongside the station on the Portsmouth side was a new bus station, which by using the pensioner bus pass provided free transport all over the city, and to places like Littlehampton and Joyce's favourite place of Chichester.

Their house was semi-detached in a mature road with all the houses having been built in or around the early nineteen-thirties. They had decorated it brightly, due to the fact that the house did not naturally let in lots of light. They were lucky in one way that there was a small park opposite, giving them a rather nice outlook from the front of the house. Whilst in theory they could get a car off the road, the driveway to their garage was shared with next door. Few in the road chose to demonstrate their driving skills, or indeed lack of them, negotiating between the walls of their houses to garages that were quite frankly full of other stuff, let alone a car. So the choice of convenience was that people parked on the road. There was just enough space to do this, by virtue that no houses existed opposite them, but even so, Hardy kept a keen eye out for 'stranger parking.' as if he had the right to deny anyone a space. It was yet another issue that irritated Joyce, yet she too would often become agitated by tradesmen parking - as she saw it - irresponsibly. It had not been unknown for her to confront such men, pointing out that people lived in the road and access was required. Her voice was always the problem; she went into a higher key when agitated and that had the effect of 'winding blokes up', while Hardy on the other hand, because of his slow drawn-out calm way of talking, had the opposite effect.

Both Joyce and Hardy drove, but there was only one car between them. Joyce identified that as yet another issue to be resolved and along with that, if they had a car each, then the parking issue would raise its head.

Their furniture was a mixture of stuff they had bought for the house they were in now, and stuff that came from previous dwellings. "Unlike the young" Joyce would say, "you don't throw things out just because you have moved."

Hardy's view had been different: "You do if it doesn't bloody fit." But the house was reasonable in both their eyes. There was limited space in what was a galley kitchen, and although they had a small table in it, there would be no room for a third person (not that that ever happened) to get through. The bedrooms were square and featureless, sporting only the intrusion of a chimney-breast as any variation from the square. It wasted no end of space, thought Hardy, but they had decided to leave it because it transported fumes from the gas fire in the lounge outwards to the air, and also to remove it was a ridiculous amount of money and effort.

Despite the obvious difficulties, Joyce was beginning to entertain the idea that cohabitation was the way forward. When one of them died, the value of the house would still be available to the survivor and as she was convinced that this was going to be her, then she should have due cognisance to safeguard the asset. The biggest question was who would live upstairs and who would be down. For the person downstairs, because there was only one front door, a certain amount of privacy would be compromised as the other party came into the hall to get to the stairs. That was also true, pointed out Hardy, for the one living upstairs, whose movements would indirectly be monitored by the 'gatekeeper' downstairs. The creaking floorboards indicating movement, the sounds of a TV programme, differing from the one being viewed downstairs ... lots of issues like that needed thinking about.

It was all proving somewhat of a roller-coaster for Joyce: one moment she was up, thinking this would work and it would be easy, the next she was down when considering all the problems to be resolved and the perceived inevitable intransigence of Hardy.

CHAPTER 11

How different, thought Ken. The group were now waiting on the pontoon yet again for the ferry to return from the Portsmouth side, and sitting next to Ken was a weary-looking young woman, who made him feel uncomfortable. Quite unlike the previous one, the one with the baby, with whom he felt he had struck up a relationship, this one had a young lad with her.

"Crikey, he's chatting up another one," said Olly to Sarah.

"He does seem to attract them, doesn't he?"

The new girl constantly bellowed instructions to the young lad, often inserting Anglo Saxon expletives. Ken did not like it. To him the behaviour represented what he disliked most about British society today. There was a sort of commonness, a banal and base attitude that seemed to prosper in all areas in Britain. If Ken sat in a restaurant and a group of three or more young people came in, he would argue that you could put money on the fact that they would quickly become loud and disturbing, with bad language and a genuine discourtesy to those around them. This woman seemed the perfect example of everything he disliked.

Ken could clearly hear the conversation that was going on between them. She was then joined by a man who looked like he had the tickets.

"Moody sod!" she had exclaimed to this new arrival.

"Oh, come on, he's fourteen, it's a hormone storm." The man, who seemed much older than her, was obviously trying to calm things down. He started to point out that it was difficult for the boy.

"Look, you and I are in a new relationship, I've only been going out with you for three weeks, and your boy is probably confused and angry, trying to work out who I am and whether I pose a threat to him.'

Ken had worked out that they were called Mike and Mandy, but apart from 'moody sod' he could not ascertain the name of the lad. People seemed either to meet at work now or online, with just the occasional relationship blossoming from some other social interaction. This relationship probably started online, thought Ken. Mandy, he reckoned, was onto a good one here with this guy, and therefore somewhat deferred to him.

Ken was making lots of assumptions, but then he often did, in his observations of people. He had Mike down as some sort of senior manager in perhaps a tech company, and he looked at least a good ten years older than her. He reckoned that she was a single parent and preferred her men older, perhaps assuming almost a father-like role, taking charge of her life and shielding her from the responsibilities. Mike was taller than her by about 18 inches. He was sufficiently young to look a right mess in Ken's eyes, wearing trainers with those funny little socks, a pair of salmon-coloured shorts and a T-shirt that was, in Ken's view sporting an inappropriate sentiment regarding meeting a girl and getting her into bed. Even though he must be in his early forties, Ken guessed, you would think he would have grown up a bit by now. The thing that always amazed Ken was that the sort of clothing Mike was wearing probably cost more than a tailored suit.

Mandy had obviously had enough of 'the moody sod', suddenly leaving her seat and rushing over to him, shouting at the top of her voice to stop swinging on the railings.

Mike was clearly finding the shouting and language embarrassing and left her and the boy to perch his backside on one of the slightly angled seats now available next to Ken.

"Bit of a handful?" Ken proffered to him.

"Yeah, to be frank it's pissing me off." Well that was 'frank', thought Ken.

Mike continued: "The boy is damaged – not his fault – but she's completely out her depth with him. 'Course, I've not been with her for that long, but I'm already being regarded as both a meal ticket and as someone to put things right with the boy. Trouble is, the boy hasn't a clue as to whether he's coming or going."

"Very difficult," Ken agreed. He wondered why in just the space of a few minutes he was now the sounding board for yet another person. Mike went on to tell him more.

"She and her ex had screwed up. She's told me that she had continually frustrated him and ignored him, which eventually erupted into violence, and then Dan – that's her ex – left her and Gavin."

So 'moody sod's name was Gavin, noted Ken.

"She hasn't heard a word from him since that night. He gave her a right-hander to her jaw and dislocated it, but she lied to the hospital: said she'd fallen and caught her face on the corner of a chair. She wasn't sure the medical staff believed her, but they were stretched with other work, so just let it go. At that point she believed Dan would come back and that this was the 'air clearer' and that they could sort it."

"Did he come back?"

"Only to collect his stuff – and he did that while she was at work and Gavin was at school. I reckon it was that then that it dawned on her that the marriage was really over. She was only nineteen when they got married and she lost touch with friends because of it – they were out clubbing and she was staying in, saving for a house they might buy in the future."

"That's weird, isn't it?" commented Ken, "She doesn't come across as someone who would save for a house."

"No she doesn't. Maybe it was Dan's idea. Anyway, after a year of marriage she was bored. One of her old friends at work was having a leaving 'do' in a local wine bar. She had invited Mandy, although Dan said it was a waste of money, she had gone anyhow.

"She'd bought something new to wear – a mini skirt and stuff. I dunno: she might have looked a bit tarty, to be honest."

Ken knew what he meant.

"She told me she'd been nervous because she'd not been out to a social event in a couple of years, and then it had been with Dan. She couldn't remember when she had last been out in her own. So she drank too much and the evening had become a bit of a blur. The others all went on to an Indian restaurant, but she decided against it and got a taxi home.

It was only about nine o'clock but there was a row when she got in. Dan questioned her relentlessly on who had said what to her, and what had been her response. She was furious. After all, she'd come home – she could have gone on and had a really good time she told him – but instead had come back home to him."

"Yeah," said Ken, "but that seems to be nearly normal these days that wives and girl friends go out on their own, just the same as the men do."

"True, but Dan was livid. He said what she was wearing made her look like a slut, not a happily married woman. But she was young and naïve. She had stormed off to bed and had told him to piss off. He got more and more paranoid after that, convinced she was seeing other blokes.

"After he broke her jaw and ran off, the reality that she was free took several weeks to dawn. It was not what she had wanted in the first instance, she told me, but the more she thought about things, the more she realised that she'd had a lucky escape. The big downside was Gavin: he missed his dad and she could not console him. She never tried to turn Gavin against him, though. Whenever they talked about it, her answer to everything was always "Shit happens." Dan made no effort to contact either of them again. Time just drifted by, and Gavin got to know a number of 'uncles'."

Ken made a sympathetic noise.

"Oh yes," said Mike, "I know that I am far from special, and can easily be replaced. Anyway, Mandy went out most Saturday nights and Gavin was left to look after himself. She always had her mobile on her, she had said, and if there was any problem he was to ring her."

"Well I suppose that's better than nothing." Ken was feeling bewildered by the way Mike was opening up to him – a total stranger. Like with the girl earlier, this was not normal. In fact nothing happening today was normal, he thought.

"For Gavin, life got worse. His best friend at school said to him that his mum was 'putting it about'. Gavin then hit him and that was the end of the friendship. Gavin became increasingly withdrawn: he just stayed in his room all the time – even took his meals up there.

"It was on his fourteenth birthday that the big surprise happened: a card landed on the mat. It was from his dad and just read 'love you son, have a good day, Dad'. Gavin now thought that his dad was being prevented from seeing him and the idea festered. He began to see his mother as another person who letting him down."

"Poor sod." Ken could only imagine the mental turmoil the boy must be in. He glanced over to the railings, where Mandy, hands on hips, was still berating the lad.

"I'd like to think I might bring a bit of stability to their lives," said Mike. "But it's early days: I just fancied her something rotten – I didn't anticipate being a kind of social worker to her kid. I'm not sure it's what I really want long-term."

"Well I wish you the best of luck, mate," Ken responded with a note of cynicism.

Now, on the pontoon, she was still shouting at Gavin. She was not the sort of fellow traveller that Ken wanted. He found the language distasteful, angry and vengeful, and this was being played out in public. He found it difficult these days to recognise much at all in the world: perhaps that was one of the reasons he found himself in this ridiculous position.

"Won't be long until he's drug dealing, put money on it," said Mike despondently.

"Really?" enquired Ken, more out of curiosity that anything else.

"Well he won't see any future in anything else. He'll be able to make big cash that way, and quickly.

The encounter had made Ken think. Every generation seemed to have a set of problems unique to itself. He thought back to when he was fourteen. It was a time of The Beatles and The Rolling Stones and – according to the newspapers – every teenager was having a great time apart from him. Every boy in the class seemed to be shagging just about every girl in the town apart from him. He was getting up at six in the morning to deliver newspapers in the pouring rain. There was the pressure of GCEs - you couldn't do anything in life without GCEs, he was told. He had achieved two, one in Art and one in Religious Instruction. That was sufficient enough to label him 'not thick', but the label of 'intelligent' was not applicable.

He played football, and it had been so important to be selected for the school team: when he wasn't, he was devastated.

Ken had moved away from Mike and found himself talking now with Sarah and Kenneth.

"Bit of an eye opener that, you know."

"What?"

"That boy over there."

"Vandal, isn't he? Takes no notice of his mother at all."

"You're right, and she is beside herself not knowing what to do. She can't seem to provide any security for the lad, or provide any role model whatsoever."

"Who is the guy?" Sarah asked. "Is he not the dad?"

Sarah was always impressed at how much Ken would establish about people just by observing and listening. But then that, to be fair, was part of his job.

"He's new to them: the boy's father has left after an altercation with the mother."

"Huh, typical!" said Kenneth to Ken, "No staying power. What do they call them? 'Snowflakes' isn't it?"

"Yeah, maybe, but when you hear of the stuff going on in their lives, I doubt whether we would have done much better. I mean we never had the constant pressure of the internet for a kick-off. This Facebook thing and Snap something-or-other, twenty-four hours a day seven days a week, messages all the time, people telling you they've a better phone than you, or that they are going some place today, or that they have a new something-or-other, just creates envy all the time. Do you know they even photograph their breakfast some days so that their friends can envy that as well?"

"I'm on Snapchat," said Sarah.

"Are you?" exclaimed Ken.

"Didn't know that," said the other Kenneth.

"And then there's drugs." Ken had not finished comparing life now with life then. "Stupid things like the only numbers my mother needed to make me remember was my house number and her Co-op number, so she got her 'divvy' every six months."

"Oh yeah, I remember that, depending on how much you spent you got some money back. Had to go to an office, and just about everyone else you knew in the town was there getting there four shillings and twopence or something like that."

"And didn't it make them happy? Didn't it make them feel rich for just a day or so? Then do you remember the man would come and empty the gas and electric meter, that for what seemed an eternity you had stuffed with shillings and then he would leave a big pile of them on the mantelpiece as a rebate."

"So what you are saying, Ken?"

"Well ..." He sounded almost defeated. "None of those little things happen now. What has she got to look forward to, or what has the boy got to look forward to? It seems that we have completely changed life as we have gone along over the past fifty years. People were born to love each other, and buy stuff to be used, but now they love stuff and use people. We should reach out to them, but I suspect the hand that reaches will be ignored, don't you?"

Neither Kenneth nor Sarah actually answered him, being a little unclear of his point.

The green-and-white ferry was now doing its usual 'skid' towards the pontoon. In a matter of seconds it would be alongside, passengers disembarking at one end and embarking at the other. No one ever charged the gate. It was one of the most polite situations one can imagine; no one pushed or barged to get on, and no one hurried because there was no point. You just could not hurry the Gosport Ferry. It would get you all onboard, and might even wait for others, but hard luck if it was time to go, because that was what it would do – go – and that was why many people in Gosport were fast enough to run the one hundred metres in an Olympic Games.

CHAPTER 12

Olly's heart was thumping; he could feel it in his chest, which was reasonable, he thought, because that is where the heart was located.

This compared with Hardy's heart, which was only just beating. Hardy was wandering into this exciting adventure with not much recognition of what was going on. If he spoke the truth, this thing didn't really matter now - nothing really mattered.

Before they had entered the pontoon to await the ferry, Hardy had told Joyce he was going to find a loo. He did. He found it in The Castle Inn just fifty yards from the Falkland Gardens. He ordered a double scotch, transgressing his lifetime mantra of never mixing the grape with the grain. He used the loo and the scotch awaited his return, on the bar. It took him all of thirty seconds to down it and it quickly rejuvenated his alcoholic bliss, sidelining the world's worries, and even making Joyce appear attractive again.

Before leaving, he debated whether he should have another, just to keep him going. He did, only this time ordering a single. He looked at the glass - he could only just see the scotch covering the bottom. The lesson, as just about all drinkers understand, was that a measure served in a public house or bar was quite quite different from what you would pour yourself at home.

"Bloody hell," he said to the landlord, "Is that all you get for a single?"

"It is, buddy, not much is it?" Hardy hated this term used a lot in Gosport – 'buddy.' What did it mean? It seemed to have taken over from 'mate' as a term of male endearment, yet another sign of American influence he thought.

Hardy knew that the measure was right. He related a story to the landlord, who at first seemed uninterested but did indeed chuckle at the end.

"Several years ago, my cousin was asked by her niece to supervise a pub that her niece and husband were running during their absence on holiday. My cousin and her sister were not meant to do anything - there was staff for that - but just to live upstairs and look after the dog and whatnot. The thing was: she was a dyed-in-the-wool Salvationist and of course they don't touch alcohol. But she was not the sort of person that objected to pubs and people drinking in moderation. It was those men who drank the pay packet before they got home and had nothing to give to starving families, and brought about social ruin … you know what I mean.

Well anyway, she and her sister decided to take the dog for a walk one lunchtime, and to do so had to pass the rather crowded and busy bar. Well, she decided to help and offered to serve one of the customers who asked for a whisky. "Which one is that" she asked. Well the gentleman pointed to the Bells, and she pushed the glass up to the optic. That was going to cost this man three pound something. Can't be right, she thought, this piddly little bit in the bottom, so she proceeded to give him another shot. The gentleman shouted that he only wanted a single, but my poor cousin could not believe that she had to charge him that much money for a dribble in the bottom of the glass. She only ever did charge him for one, but what a lovely lady to be served by, eh?"

"Depends which side of the bar you're on, sir, don't it?"

Hardy had made the point, he thought. Daylight robbery, but the measure was sufficient to do the trick and he rejoined the others on the pontoon as the ferry nudged the pontoon to take a new lot of seafarers on board.

Joyce had looked at her husband upon return. He queried to himself: "is she looking at me with suspicion or am I just transplanting my guilt on to her?" She never said anything, and nor did any of the others, so he must be carrying this wonderful feeling off without anyone noticing.

Olly by now had taken charge. Olly found it difficult to judge just how much Hardy had consumed. Hardy's reddened cheeks, the odd way his eyes were focusing, the speech even more slurred than normal, certainly indicated that he had consumed enough, but there was no gauge to tell the others that he had 'topped up' in the last five minutes. In his heart, Hardy was not proud about this habit. He kept telling himself it had to stop. He did not crave alcohol normally, but when he had consumed one or two then he couldn't stop. In a way, and this was his excuse, it crowded out the 'horrible' world in which he found himself. The problem was that, as nice as things seemed when he went to bed, he always woke up to the same old world. The relief was only temporary.

Joyce never took charge of his drinking at home, but she always made Hardy aware that he had consumed sufficient in her eyes. Hardy drank most evenings now, particularly since Joyce had made the announcement of the divorce proceedings. He never really started until four or five o'clock, but Bert's invitation to brandy earlier had superseded that timeline. Once he started, he would need to keep going, otherwise that dulling sinking prospect of sobering up would creep up on him, and his earthly misery would reappear with the added bonus of drowsiness and a dull head from the alcohol. 'No,' he would tell himself, he was better off going to bed still under the influence; that way he would sleep, he would not have to face her and he would drift off easily and awake in the morning with only marginal signs of a hangover. Another night done.

He thought now, though, that perhaps he had had one too many. Was the pontoon moving up and down, or was it him? Was Joyce actually being pleasant to the ferry operative that was clipping the tickets or was this an illusion? It got to his turn. Where had he put his pensioner ticket? He stood clumsily searching his pockets. Men of his age had so many pockets, he thought. Others behind him waited patiently as his mood slowly changed to panic.

"Oh for God's sake!" Joyce was really addressing herself more than anyone else as she turned around to check where the silly old bugger was.

"Hardy! Hardy! I got your ticket clipped. I had it."

"Go on then, mate," the ferry crewman implored. At least it was 'mate' and not 'buddy'.

By now the pontoon seemed to be moving more than ever and the ferry, whilst close up against the pontoon, seemed to be a challenge to board.

"Are you OK, mate?" asked the smartly dressed ferry crewman. He sported a crisp white shirt with the ferry logo embroidered on the breast pocket. He also sported a wonderful moustache, something not seen so often these days, thought Hardy.

The crewman assumed that this was just one of the symptoms of getting older - that you staggered and not in a straight line either. He made sure Hardy negotiated the extremely small gap of less than two centimetres from the pontoon. He did.

This time, Joyce did eye him, properly.

"You're still drunk, aren't you?" She was not looking for an answer because she voiced her suspicions. "Or have you had more?" Joyce could not see how that could have happened, but she also knew how devious Hardy could be.

"It's actually none of your business, is it?" he slurred.

"It is when you are with me, when you are with this group and you are showing me up. That makes it very much my business, Hardy."

"They're at it again," observed Sarah.

"Well, he's pissed - look at him, pissed as a newt," Ken informed her.

Sarah was not good at spotting such conditions and just accepted Ken's word for it; after all, Ken was a man of the world.

Olly was heading upstairs to the open deck at the top. To the front end of the deck was a raised bridge from which the ferry was steered and manoeuvred. The Captain occupied the bridge now, and soon as they left the pontoon the two assistants would join him on the bridge. They had two stools on the bridge on which they sat for two minutes as the boat ploughed its way towards Portsmouth. One then would go to the stern to tie up as it reached the Portsmouth pontoon, whilst the other would go to the bow end. One would see the passengers safely off, while the other started to take the tickets of those embarking on the journey to go the other way. The journey was approximately four minutes; slightly longer if the ferry was obliged to wait for a yacht or go to the stern of some bigger ship making its way in or out of the harbour. In that case you would get the excited shrieks of small children as the wake of a bigger ship made the ferry bounce. Hardy was hoping that would not happen.

Bounce for Hardy in his current condition would be bad news.

Even without a 'bounce' the steps to the upper deck also provided Hardy with a challenge.

Ken remembered earlier in the day the trouble getting Bert up there; he certainly had no wish to repeat the performance.

"Is that a good idea, mate?" a fellow passenger queried when he saw the state Hardy was in trying to climb the steps.

It was pathetic. Hardy came out with the same stuff that they had used that morning for Bert; he was ill and wanted to see the glorious Portsmouth Harbour one more time. This story interested the passenger, who volunteered to help Hardy up the steps.

Joyce was by now incandescent with rage.

"The bastard!" she exclaimed.

"And to come out with that rubbish as well, when poor Bert this morning was actually ill. Hardy is the biggest bastard I know." Who she was actually addressing, no one seemed to know and to be fair, no one seemed to care.

"What on earth do you lot think you are doing?" Whilst the Captain was undoubtedly annoyed, he also carried a sparkle in his eye that indicated slight amusement.

"This is a protest." Hardy was speaking quickly by his standards - after all, this was the culmination of hours of planning. He was full of Dutch courage now, but to be honest, he felt the effects of the brandy and scotch were wearing off already, and he was just detecting the 'down' feeling, which if he had been at home he would have anticipated by slipping down another shot of something. He thought that just one more was all he needed to really pull this off.

He had done it, however - he had got this far He had previously contacted the *Portsmouth News*, who were no doubt taking pictures from the other side at this very moment. Joyce had contacted them from her mobile some twenty minutes before they embarked, hopefully giving them enough time to arrive at Portsmouth Hard.

The Captain was smartly dressed in white shirt, black tie and black trousers. There was no doubt he had authority. Hardy always thought you should look the part. The Captain actually looked like a Captain and hence received the respect he deserved. Hardy was always saying that standards of dress had deteriorated, not just among ordinary people, but in organisations like the Royal Navy, police and nurses. You had a job to distinguish a nurse from a cleaner these days, and sailors were walking around in public in what was known as 'number eights' a dress for working in. All rigs were numbered in the Royal Navy. But the guys on the Gosport ferry looked 'proper' in his book. Hardy always referred to an interview years ago on a Michael Parkinson show, when he was interviewing some chap that had been in the film Somebody's List. This actor had been required to play the part of a Nazi officer, and when he got into the uniform, he had found that subconsciously he had started strutting around in a very upright manner. By donning the uniform, he had said, he had become that Nazi officer. Olly's problem was that whenever Hardy related something like that, he could not put names to people: it was always someone called 'what his name' and so lost a little of the credibility.

"You're meant to get off after every journey," the Captain informed them. "There are several notices to that effect all over the ferry."

"You don't understand, do you?" Olly was taking over

now and had become earnest again. "This is a protest, and as protestors we do things like this, like not getting off after each journey."

"Yeah." Hardy associated himself with the statement. He had to keep in contact with this action – this was so important to him yet he could feel it slipping away, not being really in charge and with only himself to blame.

"Well, how long are you thinking of staying on here then?"

"What's the time now?"

"Ten to four."

"Is it as late as that? Well … I suppose we will be off by five."

"Most certainly," said Ken. "Sarah and I like Eggheads, we've got to be home for Eggheads, haven't we Sarah?"

Sarah nodded. There was not a lot else she could do or say at that point that would help the situation.

"And I need to get back for Helen." Kenneth felt he should get that in as well.

Sarah decided to elaborate a little. She felt that in comparison with Kenneth's quite valid excuse, hers and Ken's seemed a bit lame. "Oh yes, we saw Kevin Ashman live you know, in the Discovery Centre, right here in Gosport."

Kenneth also felt the compulsion to re-emphasise his need to leave, pointing to the fact that he too had certain deadlines based around medication for his wife, and that he had told his wife that he would not be late.

Sarah filled what she perceived to be a void in the conversation. "You see, Olly, marriage doesn't just end when one of you dies. It can't do – you are too close. You are like a foot in a slipper – one without the other isn't that warm, so take comfort that you are together forever."

Olly looked at her blankly. What rubbish was she on about? Where did that come from and for what reason?

It wasn't even a great speech, but it terrified Hardy, who had overheard even though he was close to dosing off yet again. You mean you can't even escape your wife in death.

Ken went over to Olly. "It's strange, Olly - she does this every so often, comes out with stuff that I can't make head nor tail of."

To his relief, the Captain saw that there was an end to this occupation, and all he had to do was to play the time game, speaking of which he needed to get the ferry back over to the other side.

Hardy assured the Captain that they would not make any trouble, indeed he and his wife were going to get off anyway when they reached the Portsmouth side, so that they could deal with questions from the press. But he decided to reinforce his insistence that the others would not get off when they berthed, and would return to Gosport with the banner still on display.

"The company will no doubt charge you for this," said the Captain. "You can't keep riding backwards and forwards as if you were on a pleasure cruise, you know."

"Oh of course, we will pay our fares and remove the banner before we get off." said Hardy.

Olly was concerned at this: this wasn't how protestors work, but he decided not to make an issue of it in front of the Captain, who by now was bemused by the whole affair.

Ken sported beads of sweat on his brow from the effort of fixing the banner. He had found bending over the railings difficult and was searching for breath when he eventually came up. There must have been a dozen or so passengers sitting on the upper deck. The passenger numbers at that time of day were not high going to Portsmouth, but heavier coming back to Gosport as people returned from work and school. The passengers appeared to be not taking much notice of anything. There were considerably more now waiting on the Portsmouth pontoon as time plodded on towards the evening rush hour.

"What are you protesting about anyway?" the Captain eventually asked.

"The fact that you are not part of the bus pass scheme - you can see that from the banner."

Indeed, one could read quite easily through the railings:

BUS PASS FOR FERRY PENSIONERS

Bert had done a great job with the painting, creating shadow around the letters. There was little room for anything else because in order for people to read it, the letters had to be large.

Hardy intended to get his point over more forcibly when interviewed by the *News* and no doubt BBC 'South Today' would be waiting. He intended to get off to do the interviews and then join the others for the final trip back to Gosport, before Ken and Sarah departed for Eggheads, and Kenneth departed to be with his wife. He and Joyce would be left to deal with the publicity things on their own, and then travel back on their own, not exactly what they had planned, but then whole day had not exactly gone to plan.

There was indeed a reporter waiting for them. She looked no older than sixteen and whilst very attractive, with wavy blonde hair and shapely figure, it somewhat disappointed Hardy that a more senior figure was not sent to cover such an important story.

She had taken some photos herself and now wanted one

of Hardy, who readily agreed. He was waking again; this 'girl' was worth waking for. Joyce had seen him many times make a fool of himself with younger women and was always embarrassed by it. Joyce wanted to be in the picture as well. She was also concerned that Hardy was looking really rough by this point, the effects of the 'alcohol poisoning' as she called it now attacking his body and facial looks with a vengeance. Even though temporarily he had felt great, he certainly didn't look it now.

"Why did you have to get off the ferry with me as well? It only requires one of us."

"Indeed it should only require one of us, but you can't handle anything like this - I will deal with the press, particularly with the state you are in."

Hardy would always rise to her rebukes. He then noticed that Olly had got off with them as well, again not part of the plan, but Olly was insistent that he was not prepared to leave the press conference to a drunken Hardy and an angry Joyce.

"So who is the leader of this protest? It's me, isn't it?" Hardy made a stake for his power.

"For these purposes, I am. I am the press officer," said Joyce.

The reporter seemed confused. Olly pointed out in a confidential manner to the reporter that Hardy had 'had a few'. She seemed to find this amusing rather than being disgusted like Olly and the others. Olly made the assumption that the young have different perceptions of what is funny and what is not.

"The press officer!" Hardy was incredulous. "How long have we had a press officer?"

"Since now, since it required a professional to deal with the press. Remember, I am trained."

Hardy doubted that she had been trained. He remembered her doing a one-day course on press releases in connection with the motorbike club, but never anything more than that. But he realised this was not the time to argue; it could destroy the story, with headlines like "Group split over message". So as usual he shut up and drifted off again, studying the contours of this young blonde reporter.

"OK, well, I guess it doesn't matter who actually is the leader, I really just want a statement from you as to why you think cannabis should be legalised. Is the intention to legalise it for medical purposes or for general use too?" asked the reporter.

Hardy stared at her, as did Joyce and Olly.

They surely had misheard, so eventually Hardy offered a bewildered "What?"

"Well," she continued, "it would have been helpful if you had a pre-written statement to give me, but seeing as you have not done that, I'll just make a few notes. It is good copy to find a group of pensioners who want to legalise cannabis."

She had asked it again. Hardy had heard how the press sensationalise things and twist things to sell papers, but this would be verging on the ridiculous, even for the *News*.

Olly was totally confused. He raised his hands to his face as if at prayer. This line of questioning had to be stopped. No one was campaigning for the legalisation of anything. They wanted the ferry to be included in the bus pass scheme.

"Sorry," Joyce eventually uttered, "I am not following you - we have never said anything about legalising … what is it again?"

"Cannabis, smoking pot. I mean don't get me wrong, I'm right with you, and I suspect a lot of the public will be, so this is a great story."

"Look, hang on here, we are not protesting about cannabis, we want the ferry company to join the bus pass scheme."

"Yes, I'm sure you do, but the story is the cannabis angle."

Joyce and Hardy were now more united than at any time during the day, in their confusion.

The ferry was behind them, about to depart yet again for Gosport. They turned to check that the others were waving flags and shouting like they should be. Alas, only Kenneth was waving a chequered flag, there was no shouting, and the other Ken was talking yet again to the Captain, this time plainly engaged and laughing together. And then, there it was, as plain as day. The banner from this side read:

LEGALISE CANNABIS NOW!

Underneath it read 'Young Liberal Democrats Demand Reform'.

Hardy prodded Joyce. "Look!" he said.

She looked, turned, and then looked again.

"Oh my God!" she said. "What on earth … oh for God's sake Hardy, this is ridiculous – how on earth did this happen?"

It was the turn of the reporter to be bewildered this time, in fact bewilderment seemed to be the mood of the moment for all of them. Olly felt his legs go weak: never in all his life had he suffered such embarrassment and incompetence.

A response was required - they had called the press and the press in turn needed a story, and a story they were going to get. Hardy needed to say something, or at least garble something incomprehensible. Joyce washed her hands of the whole affair.

Hardy did say something: "Ummm."

Olly realised that it was no good standing there on the entrance to the pontoon looking like rabbits caught in a headlight. The rest of the world was going about its business, with the public now streaming onto the pontoon in droves, concerned only with their journey home. In reality, few noticed the banner. They mainly had their heads into mobile phones or were busy talking to the person next to them. Why would they be looking at a departing ferry that they had just missed? Nothing ever unusual happened on the Gosport Ferry - there was just no need to observe it because the next one would be along in a few minutes. So Olly needed to think quickly and come to the rescue. Hardy was not capable of thinking quickly when sober, let alone in the state he was in. Joyce was incandescent with rage again, and little concerned in dealing with this issue, more focused on how she was going to wreck revenge on her long-suffering husband. Eventually, Olly spoke up:

"While some of us believe in the legalisation of the drug, our main aim today was to bring to the attention of the public the high cost for pensioners to travel on the Gosport Ferry. Lots of pensioners have to use it when they attend Queen Alexandra Hospital for out-patient appointments and when visiting loved ones who are in patients in the hospital. The cost becomes prohibitive." The reporter duly made notes, and also noted that the 'press officer' had stormed off, and her 'assistant' was standing there looking vacant with his mouth semi-open. His mouth, she noted unusually moist and some dribble, just a small amount, was leaking from the side. He seemed unaware of this. To the young reporter, this was bizarre and to a degree she was largely losing interest in the whole story, but still reckoned she could make something of it.

The penny was dropping with Joyce. Bert had borrowed the canvas banner from the Gosport Lib Dems and had used the back to paint their protest statement, leaving the original message available for all to see on the other side.

"The silly ol' sod," she exclaimed to herself as she paced up and down outside the entrance to the Bus Interchange. She was some thirty yards from her hurt and depressed husband, who she could see standing next to Olly and saying what looked like a farewell to the reporter. Hardy cut a pathetic sight. She could see even from where she stood that he looked broken as well as pissed. She suddenly, quite unnaturally and to her surprise, felt overwhelmingly sorry for the man: it verged on the need to protect him and perhaps even put her arm around him. He didn't deserve this humiliation. She went back over to Olly and Hardy.

"Look," she said, "let's not beat ourselves up over this – it's gone wrong, so what?"

All three looked over towards the ferry now making its way back over to Gosport, carrying their other troops who were now untying the banner.

It was unfortunate that a gust of rare wind shot across the departing ferry, with the banner now flapping and secured by one thin string. It broke loose, taken with the wind some yards from the ferry.

It landed in the sea, to which it seemed to be instantly glued. The tide was taking it out to sea at around three knots.

"Oh God," said Olly.

"Oh Lord," said Hardy.

"Bugger," said Joyce.

The message leaving British shores heading towards the

far-off French coast of Caen, was one of old-age pensioners wishing to legalise cannabis.

When the young reporter's story hit her editor's desk, he laughed. This was going to be a different headline to their usual copy of 'OAP finds missing cat' or 'Pompey to sign Libyan International'. The story went national but not for the 'right' reasons. Joyce became somewhat of a celebrity, but not for the 'right' reasons. The church was disgusted, unaware of the mix-up: fancy encouraging the young to get off their heads! The local council was forced into saying whether they backed her or not - they didn't.

Joyce had her hair done just about every other day. She looked more and more blonde and golden for her numerous interviews, which she always tried to steer away from cannabis.

"No" she had never smoked it. She could not and would not vouch for anyone else, least of all her husband. She knew that Hardy, many years ago, had dabbled with smoking cannabis and had also tried LSD, which she reckoned was responsible for him being so slow and dozy now. Even just three years ago, he had hallucinated and ended up sheltering under the stairs in the cupboard from his long dead family that had come to kill him. She did not want to tell any of those stories, nor deny them. They had a story going here, and at least temporarily she had forgotten the scheme for them to live separately.

"Oh for God's sake Hardy, keep a sense of mystery – you need not say one way or the other, and that keeps the press interested." She did not want this to end.

Hardy never did buy a light bulb for Bert on that day. It was three days later when he did remember. Of course, Bert did not answer the door.

"Are you a friend of his?" enquired his neighbour, a lady in her seventies.

"Yes, I am. I've got him a light bulb for his toilet."

"Oh I see, so you don't know then?"

"Don't know what?"

"I had to go in last night – I hadn't seen him in several days. Well, I don't know how close you are to him but we found him dead at his kitchen table."

Hardy felt himself go cold.

"Oh bloody hell. Was he …? I mean was …? Did he have a brandy bottle in front of him?"

"Why, yes he did - is it yours?"

"No but I had been drinking it with him. He must have died that afternoon."

"They're still not sure of time of death. You better let them know."

"Who are they?"

"Just a minute." The neighbour went indoors and produced phone numbers and names which she asked him to contact. Hardy would do his duty by Bert, without doubt.

The group met a week later in Bobby's, an Italian restaurant in Stoke Road. It fell to Hardy to propose a toast to Bert. Most of the group had known him for a short while, although he had been a member of the church for as long as could be remembered.

Joyce raised her glass and made a speech: "To the very end, Bert was loyal to his friends. On that very last day of his life, he had to be forced to abandon our project, and it is with great sadness that he has not seen the enormous success that the project has produced for us. Bert is with us,

I know - I can feel it. May God bless you Bert and take you into His flock."

"To Bert." They raised their glasses.

Kenneth's wife Helen had been taken into hospital during the afternoon of the 'adventure'; unable to reach any of her medication, she had called her next-door neighbour, who panicked and called an ambulance despite her protestations that it wasn't needed and that she was sure that Kenneth would be home soon. She waited for three hours in A & E before Kenneth arrived.

Joyce and Hardy had been booked to appear on the *One Show* and Olly had been invited to stand for council by the Liberal Democrats.

Sarah was under investigation for fraud, and the affair with Ken was blown into the open. It was juicy copy for the local press, once they had linked Sarah and Ken with the demonstration and a local political party. Affairs, fraud, and demonstrations, it didn't get better. Ken argued that they were both free agents and that they were entitled to a liaison but remembered that the press never let the facts stand in the way of a good story.

When he wasn't thinking about it, the name of the girl on the bench came to him. He had known it was familiar and should ring bells – and now it did. He wished it hadn't.

As for Kenneth, he just continued dreading every knock at the door.

*****

If you enjoyed An Incident on the Gosport Ferry, then you'll also enjoy Going Over the Water, a lively history of the ferry, as told by the people of Gosport and Portsmouth. Compiled by David Gary and published by Chaplin Books: available direct from the publisher.

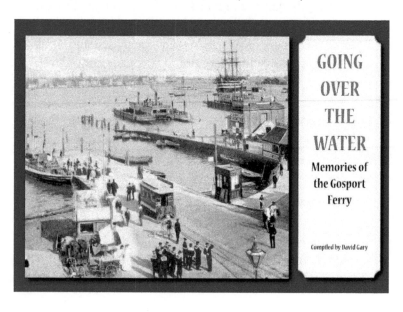

GOING OVER THE WATER

Memories of the Gosport Ferry

Compiled by David Gary

Lightning Source UK Ltd.
Milton Keynes UK
UKHW021351071220
374769UK00016B/1483